# THE MOUNTAIN MAN'S MAIL-ORDER SURPRISE

## IRON CREEK BRIDES BOOK 1

### KARLA GRACEY

*This book is dedicated to all of my faithful readers, without whom I would be nothing. I thank you for the support, reviews, love, and friendship you have shown me as we have gone through this journey together. I am truly blessed to have such a wonderful readership.*

# CONTENTS

# CHARACTER LIST

- **Katy (Katherine) White**. Blonde hair, green eyes, tall for the era, thin as a rake at the start, but fills out once in Iron Creek.
- **Garrett Harding** (Chippewa/Ojibwe name: Waabshkizi-Mnidoo). Dark brown hair, brown eyes, tall, permanent stubble, lean and wiry build, but strong.
- Zaagaasikwe (Zaaga) Garrett's Indian foster mom. Long dark hair, dark brown eyes, very wise.
- Aandeg, Zaagaasikwe's father.
- Jacob White, Katy's first husband.
- Mrs. Statham, boarding house owner in Memphis.
- Mr. and Mrs. Jones, (Mam and Pa), Katy's parents.
- Mrs. Havermeier, boarding house owner in Chicago.
- Hank Wilson, postmaster Iron Creek.

- Miss Ginsberg, St Louis boarding house owner. Sister of Mrs. Statham.
- Omagakiinsikwe (Oma), Garrett's first wife (died in childbirth).
- Anonginimi (Ano), Garrett's son, died at just a few days old.
- Judd Barclay, owner of the general store. Garrett's only real friend. Also lost a wife in childbirth, though their son survived.
- Janus, Garrett's horse.
- Alec Jenks, town blacksmith.
- Diindiisi, Zaagaasikwe's natural daughter.
- Nelson Gustavson, stagecoach driver. Half Ojibwe-half Swedish.
- Mary and Hector Jellicoe and their children, Samuel and Thomas, the family who offer Katy a position. Hector runs the local paper.
- Dibikad, Garrett's oldest friend and his first wife's lover.
- Alice and Arvind Grayson, owners of the Resting Place hotel.
- Dylan Albright, a young lad that Garrett hires to help with the sheep.

# PROLOGUE

1855, Devil Track Lake, Minnesota

The hills were dark. The storm had come in fast. Zaagaasikwe spurred her horse onward, trying to outrun it. Smoke was rising from the hunting encampment up ahead. It had been a long day, and she hoped she would be safe inside her shelter by the time the rain clouds caught up with her. The winds howled, the sound almost deafening as the sky raced overhead. Her mount nickered. Zaaga patted his neck and murmured that all would be well, but the horse continued to act up as she urged him onward.

When she turned along the trackway, she realized why. An overturned wagon lay ahead of her. There didn't appear to be anyone nearby. She slowed her pace and approached cautiously. Such things weren't always safe for an Ojibwe, as the white man wasn't always the tribe's friend. Then, the sound of a small child crying rent the air. She hadn't heard it as she'd raced across the plains with the wind in her ears, but her mount clearly had and she couldn't leave a child if it needed her, no matter the potential danger to herself. Zaaga dismounted and tentatively circled the wagon.

A white man was lying a few yards from the upturned vehicle, thrown from the wagon by the force of the crash. Blood had congealed in a deep gash on his forehead. Zaaga bent over him, listening for his breath. There was none. He was dead. She offered him up to her ancestors, hoping they would help him find his way in the afterlife. She paused for a moment, then got up and peered around the canvas covering the back of the cart. Inside, a young white woman was flat upon her back, cradling a skinny boy who couldn't have been much older than three or four. The woman did not move, though Zaaga could see no obvious wounds, but the child was red-faced, tear-stained, and screaming loudly.

Zaaga picked him up and rocked him, shushing him and soothing him as she tried to see if the mother was still alive. She was not. Again, she sent up her pleas to the ancestors. Just because these people weren't of *her* people, it did not mean that they wouldn't be able to guide them to wherever it was the white man's spirits wished to go to. She would not condemn anyone to the nothingness that might greet them without such assistance.

She looked down at the boy and pushed his unruly curls back from his hot face. "So, what am I to do with you?" Zaaga asked the child. "You are all alone in this world now." He looked up at her, his eyes wide—but with curiosity, not fear. He seemed to know that she meant him no harm, and she was glad of that. But he was not of her people. And perhaps there were people somewhere expecting this couple and their young child to arrive. People who loved them.

She rummaged in the wagon, looking for a sheet she might use to make a sling to bind him up against her body so she could carry him safely on her horse. She found one in a battered wooden trunk and quickly knotted it securely around her waist and neck, cradling the child against her heart. "You stay still and quiet. We need to get to safety," she said to him. "But I also need to find out who you are. There must be someone somewhere out there to care for you. I know that the white man usually carries papers. Do you know where they might be?" The boy remained silent, putting his thumb in his mouth for comfort and sucking gently.

Zaaga continued going through the family's possessions until she found a sheaf of papers. Perhaps there would be some clue as to the family's identity in them. She couldn't read, but there were those in the tribe who could read the language of the white man, including her father, who was a much-respected member of the elder council. If there was anyone out there who might want this little boy, it was their duty to find them. All the personal effects she found as she went through the family's things, she shoved into a large carpet bag she had found. She hoped that they would shed some light on the family's identity. She took a necklace from around the mother's neck and the pocket watch from the father's vest to give to the child, then, holding the boy close against her, mounted her horse and raced homewards.

She reached the camp just as the rains began to fall,

3

pounding down upon her bare skin. Zaaga unfastened the rope halter she used to control her mount, then slapped his rump to let him know he was free to go and find shelter, pausing momentarily as he raced away into the nearby trees, then headed inside the elm bark wigwam. Her father, Aandeg, was stoking the fire in the center of the shelter. With his almost-black hair and sharp nose, he looked every inch the crow he'd been named for as a baby. He looked up as the wind caught the hide door, which flapped around loudly and slapped against the outside of the wigwam. "I am glad to see you, my daughter," he said, hurrying to fasten it securely. "We feared you would not make it back before the storm struck."

"I almost didn't," Zaaga admitted. She unwrapped the boy and handed him to her father. "I found this little one on the track. A wagon overturned, and his parents were both dead." Her father cradled the child tenderly and whispered soft words. "I didn't know what to do with him," Zaaga continued, "but I couldn't leave him alone there to die."

"Waabshkizi-Mnidoo," Aandeg whispered over and over to the child as Zaaga fetched some milk and bread and put them in a pan to warm over the fire. When she had finished, she handed the papers she'd found in the wagon to her father.

"What's that you're calling him?" Zaaga asked as she took the child from her father and tried to get him to take a spoonful of the soft, comforting concoction.

"White Spirit," Aandeg said with a doting smile as he watched his daughter. She'd not shown much maternal instinct before now, but as she patiently fed the infant, he could see that she would be a wonderful mother when her time came.

But heaven help any man who expected her to be just a mother. Her hunting skills, sharp intelligence, and fierce passion would be stifled should they even try. Aandeg fully expected her to become a medicine woman, though that, too, was a role traditionally reserved for men. Zaaga was not the type to let that bother her, though; she would go her own way. She always had.

He picked up the papers and began to read slowly through them. "It would appear that his name is Garrett Harding and he is almost five years old."

"Garrett Harding," Zaaga said softly. "I think I prefer Waabshkizi. And he is very small for his age, don't you think?"

"He is a skinny little thing, but he'll soon grow if he keeps eating so eagerly," Aandeg said. As he spoke, the boy smiled up at Zaaga and pulled her hand with the spoonful of food in it toward his open mouth.

"Can we find his family?" she asked her father. She continued to feed the child, cooing and caressing him tenderly. He ate hungrily.

"I'm not sure he has a family, at least not now," her father said sadly. "These papers show that his parents only recently traveled to America. They were setting out, as so many do, for a new life. I think this little one is all alone in the world now."

"Then we must raise him," Zaaga said firmly. "He shall be my son from this day forward."

Aandeg knew better than to argue.

1873, Richmond, Virginia

Salty tears poured down Katy Jones' pale cheeks. When she'd pictured this moment in her mind—and she had rehearsed it over and over, in as many different ways as a girl possibly could—she'd never imagined it going like this. Pa's face was puce, but it wasn't his rage that was making Katy cry. She'd expected him to be furious. It was Mam's reaction to the news Katy had brought to them. She had never seen her mam so sad, and she hated thinking that her mother might think less of her in any way. "He's no good," Mam said, her voice low, her demeanor defeated—as if Katy had delivered a killer blow in a war she'd not known she was fighting. "He'll only let you down."

"You go anywhere with the likes of him, don't ever darken my door again," Pa said angrily. "Jacob White isn't worth your spit, girl."

"But I love him, and he loves me," Katy said earnestly. Why couldn't they see that? Why did they not think it was enough? "He's a good man. I know you don't believe me when I say that, but he is. He'll take good care of me. You'll see. Just give him the chance to prove himself."

"No, dear," Mam said. "He won't take care of you. He's not the kind to take care of anyone but himself. Can't you see he's a drifter? He'll never settle anywhere, with anyone. He's barely been here in Virginia for a few months, and already he's itching to be away even further south. We know nothing about him or his family. And he doesn't talk of them. How can we know what to think?"

"Why does any of that matter?" Katy cried passionately.

"Why would anyone want to stay here? And who his family is means little to me. Surely what matters is who he is, that he cares for me, that he is a hard worker and has the ambition to give me a good life?"

Mam sighed heavily. "You are so young." She caressed her daughter's cheek, a tear in her eye. "And when we were as young as you, we thought that all would be well as long as we loved each other, too. But dreams take you nowhere, my girl. You need a man with his feet on the ground, not one with his head in the clouds."

Katy frowned. They could not see that Jacob's plans weren't just dreams. He had a position to go to, and there were good opportunities for him in New Orleans, much more so than here in Richmond. It galled her that her parents seemed to have forgotten that they too had been made to feel bad about their dream of coming to America to make their fortunes when they were no older than she was now.

"You and Pa are happy, aren't you? You aren't so different from us. How can you so easily forget?" Katy looked pained at the thought that her happy family might not be as happy as she'd thought. "You wouldn't change anything—and wasn't Grandpa upset at the idea of Pa bringing you here to America?"

Pa frowned. Mam hugged Katy close, her voice choked with emotion. "Oh, my darling girl. It's because we know how hard it is to be so far from family and friends that we are worried. Coming here turned out well for us, but don't for so many. And we had no choice but to seek our fortunes else-where. There was nothing for anyone in Ireland when we left.

7

You have a good position with Mrs. Clayton, and your Jacob has an apprenticeship with Mr. Smith. He's barely a year from getting his papers. To leave now would be foolish."

"But he wants to go. He is sure that his fortune lies elsewhere, and he hates being a blacksmith. He has a good position lined up, on a steamship—the Emily B. Souder. He's quick and clever and works hard. He'll rise up through the company soon enough. I know he will. And he'll be happier out on the river than trapped in a hot and sweaty forge."

Pa snorted. "Work's not for what you like or don't like," he said, shaking his head. "It's for keeping a roof over your family's head and food on the table."

There was nothing more to be said. Katy would never convince her parents that she and Jacob would be fine, that they knew what they were doing. And her parents would never understand why Katy and Jacob longed for their lives to be different, to be better. She kissed her parents' cheeks and hugged them tightly. "I'll be seeing you, then," she said sadly. "Because we'll be wed tomorrow and on our way the day after. If you change your mind, the service will be at St. Paul's at eleven o'clock. I want you to be there and would be glad of your blessing. But it won't stop me if I don't get it. I love you and hope that you love me enough to see this is what I want. Jacob and me, we'll make it work."

She looked at them sadly, picked up her suitcase, then let herself out of the house. She wondered if it was possible for something that should be such a joyous occasion to be more miserable. All her life she'd imagined Pa proudly walking her down the aisle and giving her hand to her husband, but now she feared that her family wouldn't even be in the church. Jacob was waiting for her on the street. He took one look at her sad face and embraced her. "They aren't coming?"

"I don't think so," Katy sobbed. "They think you're foolish to give up your apprenticeship when you are so close to getting your papers, and that I am a silly girl to be following you across the country, chasing false hope."

"Don't they see we're just trying to build something more for ourselves?" Jacob said fervently. "I can't imagine anything worse than shoeing horses for the rest of my life, always tied to one place. They came here from Ireland when they were newlyweds. Why do they not understand?"

"I don't know," Katy said. She wiped her tears away and exhaled loudly. "But they don't, so we are on our own. They'll not be there tomorrow."

Jacob sighed. "I took a room for you at the lodging house next door to mine," he told her. "Just in case this happened."

Katy gave him a feeble smile and tried to force her thoughts elsewhere. "I should tell Mrs. Clayton," she mused. "There'll be an even greater furor there, I'll bet. She won't give me a character reference."

"You won't need it," Jacob boasted proudly. "My new position on the paddle steamers will mean that you'll never have to work again. It's good, honest work, and well-paid. I'll never have to slave over a hot furnace again, and I'll give you a good life, I promise." He meant it, too. He was a hard worker, even when he hated his work, and he loved Katy with all his heart. Jacob had to prove to her family that he wasn't the good-for-nothing bounder they took him for.

# CHAPTER 1

*E*arly April 1878, Iron Creek, Minnesota.

The weather was harsh, but Garrett Harding didn't care. He was used to the life up here in the borders. The beauty of this magnificent landscape more than made up for the hardships it caused. He enjoyed the challenges and had never known anything different. He'd never wished to live anywhere else, even though he was unsure of where he truly belonged. As the white foster child of an Anishinaabe mother, he'd grown up feeling that he was not a full member of the tribe who had taken him in, nor of the white world he'd only come to know as an adult.

Now he tried to straddle both worlds. He could not deny that there were some situations in which being a little of both had its benefits. Garrett was perfectly placed to act as the go-between for the tribe and the local white traders. His career was lucrative and had brought a level of prosperity and security to the local Ojibwe. But though he was accepted by them, and welcomed by the white traders, he still didn't really fit with either. Although he was the child of white parents, he had been raised by an Anishinaabe woman, given an Ojibwe name, and knew no other world than theirs.

The rules and mores of the white man's world had been as alien to him as the Chippewa customs and way of living were to the people inhabiting the local white towns. He'd had to learn so much, and learn it fast, when his grandfather had started taking him on trading missions hoping his presence might be of assistance to the tribe in some way. It had been more successful than the tribe could ever have imagined, but as Garrett got more familiar with the culture that should have been his own, he'd been seduced by it and had become restless.

Garrett had welcomed friendships with those of his own kind and had wanted to learn more about the culture that should have been his all along, and so he had moved away from the tribe and into a nearby town, where he'd learned to be the man he currently was. He drank in the saloon, as his new friends did. He gambled at cards and won and lost a fortune. For a while, he had forgotten all about the people who had raised him. When he returned to trade with the Anishinaabe, he could see the pain in his mother's eyes that he had been gone so long and had changed so much. But he couldn't resist this new world that had opened to him.

And then, too late, he'd realized that his new friends weren't friends at all. They had happily picked him clean of his winnings at the card tables, having lured him in and made him think he was as good as any of them at the games they played. They'd left him without a penny to his name. Desperate to claw back something, he had continued to gamble. They took his horse and the deed to the small piece of land he'd claimed as his own, leaving him with nothing.

He had gone home to Zaaga, his tail between his legs, to nurse his wounds. But he no longer felt welcome there, either. So, when he'd managed to earn enough money, he had left once more, taking his childhood sweetheart, Oma, with him. They had traveled the length and breadth of the northern territories. He had traded successfully, and they had returned to the Ojibwe homelands from time to time. But the life was a hard one and Oma tired of it. She tired of his drinking and his gambling, and of the constant comments about his Ojibwe wife. The tensions grew between them until they eventually became too much, and Oma had decided to stay at home where she belonged. But Garrett wasn't sure whether he belonged or not. Without the answer to that question, he seemed destined to a life of wandering. It had taken a tragedy to make him reconsider things, and he would regret all that had happened back then until the day he died.

When he realized he would never feel that he fitted anywhere, he had bought a modest piece of land, enough to raise a small herd of sheep or goats, up in the mountains near a new settlement called Iron Creek, named for the red-tinged river that ran nearby and spoke of the rich iron deposits in the ground in these parts. The whole region was waking up to it, and men were flooding there to make their fortunes in the mines that supported a burgeoning iron industry in the nearby

Mesabi Range, supplying the docks in Duluth. Garrett was happy not to take that kind of gamble, though he still struggled to resist if a poker game was happening when he went into town. Raising animals for food made more sense to him, as all men needed to eat. It was safe. Good, honest work that would always pay the bills.

And he was happy up here, for the most part, alone on his little piece of the world. He'd built himself a cabin, though it was barely four walls and a roof, and he'd soon have enough money to buy a herd. Maybe then he wouldn't feel so lonely, so apart from everything and everyone. Livestock, with its noises and smells, would break the endless silence, and he'd be forced to go to market to sell the fleeces, meat, milk, and cheese. Perhaps he'd even meet someone who might consider taking him as a husband and lighten the dark nights and brighten the sunny days.

A movement a little way down the mountain alerted him to someone approaching. He smiled when he saw his foster mother Zaaga's palomino coming up the narrow pathway toward his small shack. He moved to greet her and took the horse's rope bridle to steady it as she dismounted. Even now, she rode bareback. He'd bought her a saddle once, but she'd refused to use it, so he'd taken it back and sold it. He'd put the money into his tin under the bed, adding to his savings to buy a herd with his mother's blessing.

"I am glad to see you," he said as she embraced him. "But to what do I owe such an honor?" She looked well, though there were more lines around her eyes and gray had appeared in her long raven-dark hair.

"Can a mother not come and see her son?" she said with a warm smile. "If I waited for you to come to me, I should wait until I am on my deathbed."

"You exaggerate," he said as he led her horse toward the shack and hitched it to the wooden pole outside. But she wasn't far wrong. He avoided going home to the camp these days. It was too difficult for him. There were times when he wished he'd never left—and other times when he wished Zaaga had never found him and raised him as her son. He didn't deserve his adopted people's love and affection. Garrett had done all he could to leave behind all the values his mother had taught him and had become the very thing so many of the Ojibwe despised—a white man in every way. He hated to see the disapproval in their eyes, their sadness, and knew they felt it was their fault he had become what he was now. And so Zaaga always came to him, sooner or later.

"I would have come soon," he lied. "I have to find some skins for a client in Bemidji Township, and everyone knows yours are the best in the state."

"Flattery, my son? I don't need it." She checked him over closely, looking for signs of health and happiness. He looked tired, his skin had a gray pallor to it despite his many hours in the saddle, and his eyes were dull. "You need company," she told him firmly as they stepped inside. Garrett put a kettle of water on the fire to boil. "You are not the kind of man to do well alone."

"Is any man?" Garrett joked. "None of us can take care of ourselves."

Zaaga took a seat at the small table by the fire. She rested her elbows on the table, linked her hands, and rested her chin on them. "You should take a bride. Diindiisi still hopes you will return and take her to your hearth."

"And she would make a fine wife, I don't doubt. But I think of her as a sister. You raised us that way. I could not wed her. And you should not tell untruths, Mother. Everyone knows she has eyes only for Binesi, as she should, given he is the man you and Aandeg chose for her so many years ago. I would not be surprised if they declare their intentions very soon."

"I agree. It is a blessing that Diindiisi is so fond of the match," Zaaga said with a sad smile. "And I understand why things are so hard for you, but there are other young women—of the Ojibwe or in Iron Creek—that would choose you given the chance, I am sure. You cannot continue to live this way, all alone. I worry for you, my son."

"What choice do I have?" Garrett asked as he spooned coffee into the pewter pot by the fire. "Other than my dear sister, though you claim otherwise, there are few women of the tribe...or rather, few fathers who might consider me for their daughters because I am a white man. And in town, few women would consider me because they think of me as Ojibwe."

Zaaga frowned. The kettle began to whistle. Garrett picked up a soft cloth he kept by the fireplace to lift it from its hook and poured the hot water into the coffee pot nearby. He reached for two cups and placed them on the table, then poured the rich, strong brew and pushed one cup toward his mother. "I am not a good catch," he said. He took a seat opposite her and sipped the bitter beverage.

"You could be," she said sadly. "If you could remember who you are. My son, a boy who straddles two worlds. Such a heritage could be a blessing rather than the curse you think it to be."

Zaaga blew on the coffee, then took a sip. She stared at her son and wondered how it had come to this—that he should be so all alone, so adrift from all the anchors she had tried to offer him. He was her son. He would always be a part of the Ojibwe. As far as she could tell, there was nobody there who saw him as anything other than a part of the tribe. Yet he was, and always had been, different. His white skin wasn't the problem. He had dark enough hair and had once been so tanned it was hard to tell the difference between him and the other boys, but there was always something that had made him feel an outsider.

When he had set out into the world of the white man, she had hoped he would realize that he belonged with them. But if anything, it had set him apart even more. He felt a kinship with the white men, Zaaga could not deny that, and something in his blood called him to them. Yet he could not reconcile himself to their ways. He had picked up all their worst habits and let go of all the best parts of himself for so long. She wanted him to find himself, but she worried he might not do so. And the longer he spent among the white man, the more she feared for him.

"You just want fat grandbabies," Garrett joked, trying to lighten the mood.

"I will not deny it," Zaaga said with a grin. "But it is also because you are not a loner, my Waabshkizi-Mnidoo." Garrett smiled at her use of his Ojibwe name. He'd always liked it, even though he'd sometimes felt it highlighted the difference between him and his friends, who mostly had animal names. His name described what made him different.

"I'm doing a very good impression of one," he said lightly. "I'm content enough."

"I overheard someone in the general store talking about taking an advertisement in the newspaper for a bride. Perhaps you might consider doing that if you fear that nobody locally might consider you."

"You don't give up, do you, my dear mother?" Garrett said, getting up and pressing a kiss to the top of Zaaga's head. "I…" he tailed off as his mother pulled out a sheet of paper from the ornately decorated bag she wore over her shoulder. She handed it to him.

"Aandeg wrote it. He is worried for you, too."

Garrett frowned, but he read what was on the paper.

Gentleman of Minnesota seeks friendly, brave woman with a view to matrimony. The subscriber can offer a fine home, kindness, and a good life. Good-natured and gentle, he wishes for companionship and a family. Applicants should be warm, tender, intelligent, hardworking, and affectionate.

"What is this?" he asked.

"We looked at some of the advertisements. They're all worded this way," Zaaga explained. "We tried not to make it sound too silly or to brag about things, as that is not your way. So many of them list how much money the man has, the things he will provide. It felt wrong to do that. Who you are is the reason someone should make a match with you, not what you have."

"But you say here I can offer a fine home," Garrett said, laughing now at how earnest she was about this. He gestured around the shack. "Have you looked at this place recently?"

"I have, but you can rebuild," Zaaga said firmly. "It is time you did. This is no way for you to live."

"Says the woman who still prefers to live in an elm bark shelter," he teased her.

"That is the way of our people. If you wish for that, then do it. But you seem to have chosen this as a compromise—not of the town, not of the Ojibwe. If you want a house, have a house—a good house without drafts and with a proper bedroom and a fine kitchen—not just a room with a roof. Even the Ojibwe don't live as poorly as you do. You know full well our people have been building longhouses for many generations, and even our elm bark camping shelters are better than this shack."

She had never been one to hold her tongue; Zaaga said what she meant. Clearly, his living arrangement worried her greatly. Garrett looked at the wording of the advertisement again. With a few tweaks, it might be something to at least try. He could not deny that he was lonely, that he longed for a family. Perhaps once he had a child of his own, he might finally know his own place in the world.

"Mother, you are hopeless," he said, running his hands through his hair. It was too long, and he needed to go to the barber in town to have it trimmed and to get a close shave. The stubble on his chin and cheeks was beginning to itch. "I will think on it. But do not get too hopeful for those grandchildren yet. Such a process could take many months, perhaps even years, to find the right person and establish enough of a connection for someone to cross the country to join me here."

Zaaga smiled, leaped to her feet, and flung her arms around his waist. "That you will even consider trying is enough for me, my son. I pray you will find happiness. That is all I want."

# CHAPTER 2

*L*ate May 1878, New Orleans

The humidity was like a lead blanket over Katy's thin shoulders as she stared at the certificate in her hand. The certificate that made it official. Jacob White was dead, and she was a widow. The love of her life, the man she had given up everything for, was no more. It seemed impossible, yet she knew it to be true. But how could she possibly bear such a truth? It was too great, too painful. Too tragic. She stood in a state of shock outside the hospital entrance, tears streaming down her face, completely oblivious to the world around her.

A young man barged past her. She stumbled at the impact of his body against hers, but didn't fall. She was so slight now, after too long with not enough to eat. Food had become hard to find, and the city was filled with fear. She'd not been able to stomach food since Jacob had gotten sick, and now she looked as though a stiff breeze would knock her over. The young man probably just hadn't seen her standing there so quietly, tears pouring silently down her cheeks as she wondered what on earth she should do now.

The streets were almost empty. Everyone was trying to stay safe, away from the outbreak of yellow fever that had already taken so many lives, including Jacob's. Katy did not know how she had not succumbed to the dreaded disease herself. She'd nursed her husband in his final days on this earth but had somehow emerged unscathed, though not intact. Jacob had not been the perfect husband, but he had loved her with all his heart. He had done all he could to take care of her, to make her happy, and to make up for the way her family had treated her when she and Jacob had announced their intention to wed and move to New Orleans.

She caressed her very gently swollen stomach. It was almost too early to know, but as well as the tiny protrusion of her normally pan-flat belly, she'd missed her courses and her usually tiny breasts were swollen and tender. She knew enough to know those signs meant she'd soon have another mouth to feed. With Jacob gone, and his wages from the paddleboats no longer coming in, she now had to find a way to support herself and raise the child that had been conceived in such love.

It had all happened so fast. One moment they had been happy, planning for their future. Jacob's position on the steam-boats had offered him all the opportunity he had been expecting, and he had learned his trade and been promoted quickly. He had done more than prove her parents wrong, and he'd been the perfect husband. Jacob had done everything he could to care for her, to provide for her, and to make her happy, and he had spoiled her in so many little ways. Katy knew she would never regret having chosen to spend the time she'd had with him—even if it had cost her her family.

Everything had been going so perfectly. Then the people Jacob worked with started to fall sick. The Emily B. Souder, the steamship that Jacob worked on, was the ship that saw the first cases. They'd heard rumors that it was yellow fever. It was frightening how rapidly it spread, and how soon they heard of friends who had succumbed. Soon, people they knew were fleeing the city, taking the dreaded disease with them, infecting more and more people as they tried to outrun it. She and Jacob had chosen to stay put. They had nowhere else to go and thought that they would be safer staying where they were and keeping away from others as much as possible.

Little did they know that he was already sick. They had barely made the decision to stay when his fever took hold. He had been strong and healthy before, but he was no match for the dreaded disease. The fever was the worst Katy had ever seen, and Jacob was soon barely conscious. Katy had called for the doctor, but he wouldn't even enter the house when Katy described the symptoms. He had no advice other than to keep Jacob cool and let the fever run its course. Despite his fierce stubbornness and physical strength, Jacob had lost his fight and left Katy alone in the world.

And now Katy had to think about how she might survive and bring his child into the world. It wasn't safe in New Orleans. If yellow fever could take Jacob, it would certainly take her if she were to fall ill. She did not know how she had avoided falling ill thus far. Yet she didn't know where she would be safe. She couldn't bring herself to go back to Richmond. Her parents had never so much as sent her a letter since she'd left with Jacob, though she'd written every month to tell them her news. She'd never given up hope that one day they might forgive her, but it seemed that was a hope that might never come to pass.

She returned home and counted out the meager coins left in the tin in the kitchen, then pried up the loose floorboard in the bedroom and took out the metal box where Jacob had hidden their savings. Inside, she found almost two hundred dollars. It should be enough to let her set up home somewhere new—but where? Could she even bear to go somewhere different, to start all over again? It had been so hard when they'd first arrived in New Orleans. She'd missed her family and friends so terribly, and it had taken an age to meet new people she trusted. But most of her friends were gone now, either having succumbed to yellow fever or having fled in the hope of saving their lives. She prayed they had all managed to find safe havens somewhere.

An old newspaper lay on the chair by the hearth. Katy picked it up. It was from almost three weeks ago, but she sat down and read it anyway. She needed to do something normal, and so she read the headlines and skipped the articles that had anything to do with the rapid spread of the disease, choosing to focus on everything else. But there had been little else to report, so she was left with only the "situations vacant" pages and the matrimonials.

She had always smiled at the listings of cowboys and soldiers who longed for a bride. Their advertisements were so short yet so full of hope for a happier future. She tried to imagine the places they all came from—Montana, Dakota, Utah, and Minnesota. So far apart, so far from New Orleans. Even now they brought her a little joy in a world where there was so little of it. Such hope, such possibility. A new life in a far-flung place, away from the hurt and pain.

Then it struck her. All of these men wanted a wife. And all of them lived so far away from yellow fever. Far away from Richmond. Far away from anywhere that was full of bitter- sweet memories. What if she were to reply to one of these men? She needed somewhere to go. They wished for someone to share their lives with, and she needed a father for her child. It just might be the perfect solution to her tragic predicament. None of them asked for love, just a wife. She could be that wife because there was no hope that she would ever love anyone the way she had loved Jacob.

But of course, this newspaper was old. All these men had probably found someone by now. She needed a newer paper. Katy grabbed her purse and hurried out of the door once more, covering her face and skin as best she could, and raced to the store on the corner. She purchased the most recent copy of the newspaper and hurried straight back home without stopping to talk to anyone. Inside, she bolted the door, washed her hands and face, and sat down to read the newest advertisements.

Before long, she'd chosen ten men who sounded at least respectable. She avoided those who talked of their wealth and status. Such things had never concerned her, and she'd read enough stories in the newspapers about mail-order brides finding that the promises made did not always match the realities they found. But she did not have time to be choosy. She had to get away from here, and soon—for her baby's sake. Her only real criterion was that they were as far from New Orleans as possible so she could get away from the deadly yellow fever decimating the city around her.

Taking out paper and pen, she carefully wrote to each of them, tailoring her words to theirs, in order to appeal to what they said they longed for. She was polite and tried not to say anything she might not later remember—or regret—but she chose not to mention the child she was sure was growing inside her. It was too soon to be certain, and there was much that could go wrong between now and when she might meet any of them. She had lost a child before, and that had been when she had been healthier and much happier. There was no need to get anyone's hopes up or give news of something that might rule her out at this stage.

She knew that she had to leave the city as soon as possible, so she gave each of the men she'd written to the address of a boarding house in Memphis that she and Jacob had stayed at on the way to New Orleans all those years ago. She knew that there were many people sick there, too, but it was the first stop along the way. If she stayed inside the boarding house as much as possible and avoided the streets, she would be safe enough, she hoped. Katy checked through each of the letters, making sure that she had expressed herself well and honestly, though there was obviously one glaring omission. Soon enough they were ready for posting.

She intended to leave as soon as she could, so she began to sort through her belongings. Katy packed only the most important things in a trunk and drew up a list of items that she could perhaps sell. After bundling herself back up, she took the letters and posted them, then went to a nearby store that sold second-hand items. She showed the owner her list. He tutted and frowned. "I can't give you much. There's deserted homes all over the city, so I've got my pick of such items for free," he said callously. Clearly, he didn't care that people had died so he might have access to their belongings without paying what they were worth. His attitude disgusted Katy, but there weren't many options open to her, so she bit her tongue.

"I'll take whatever you can give me," she said, knowing that even a small something was better than nothing at all. There'd not be a better offer anywhere else. He handed over a handful of bills and Katy winced to think that her life with Jacob, five years of happy marriage, had been reduced to just a few dollars. She thanked him briskly and arranged for him to collect the items within the hour. Katy stopped at the train station and booked a ticket to Memphis for the very next day. She'd stop there for a while and hope that any replies to her letters might catch up to her there. Hopefully, at least one of the men would write back and give her a more definite end point to her journey.

She wouldn't stay long, though. According to the newspaper, cases in Memphis were rising too, so she'd continue on toward St. Louis and then Chicago and rethink her plan if necessary once she got there. She'd ask Mrs. Statham, the lady who ran the boarding house, to forward anything to her. Chicago certainly had to be far enough away for her to be safe, and it would be the ideal place to travel to almost anywhere in the entire country from. If she had to, she would build a new life for herself without a man. She would be strong for her child. She had to be.

Katy could hardly sleep that night and had no appetite for breakfast before she set out the next morning. She dragged the trunk onto Jacob's old handcart, placed the large carpetbag she had packed with her day-to-day things on top of it, and headed for town.

The train station was busy with people clamoring to escape the city. She was thankful she'd had the foresight to book her ticket, as so many were turned away unable to travel. As she made her way through the station house, she walked into the fog of steam and smoke on the platform. There were no porters to be seen, so she took her trunk to the baggage car herself, leaving the handcart behind on the platform, then found her seat in the carriage. She pulled a cushion from the carpetbag and placed it on the bench, then tucked her things below the seat and out of the way.

The journey to Memphis was longer than she remembered, and her backside was numb despite the comfort of the cushion she'd had the foresight to bring. She remembered all too well having suffered from the lack of one when she and Jacob had traveled to New Orleans just a few years earlier. Of course, that journey had been a happier event, so the time had passed more swiftly. Now, every moment without Jacob dragged.

Memphis resembled New Orleans as she'd left it. Hundreds of people lined up outside the station trying to get away, but the streets were eerily quiet everywhere else. The people who had no choice but to stay—or who refused to leave—had shut themselves up inside their homes. Katy wondered how far the disease had spread and when she would no longer feel the fear of its presence.

She made her way to Mrs. Statham's. Under the current circumstances, the elderly woman would probably be reluctant to take her in—if she was even still in Memphis—but Katy wasn't above playing on the fact she was pregnant to gain sympathy and a bed for a few nights. She rapped on the door and waited for a response. There was none. For a moment, Katy feared that the elderly woman might have chosen to leave the city, perhaps to join her sister, who Katy recalled lived in St. Louis. Then she heard a movement behind the door. "Mrs. Statham, it's me, Mrs. White," she called. "Please open the door."

The door inched open cautiously, and the pale and thin face of the once kindly landlady peered nervously out, her eyes darting about to see if there were others nearby that she should be afraid of. "I'm not taking guests," Mrs. Statham explained. "It's not safe—and you've come from New Orleans. No, I can't." She looked at Katy with wide eyes, her hands clasping and unclasping in an agitated way.

"Mrs. Statham, please," Katy begged. "I've lost my husband to this disease—nobody knows its dangers more than

I. But I'm pregnant and have nowhere else to go. I just need a couple of nights. I shall stay in my room. I will not go anywhere. I promise."

"Mrs. White, I just can't." The older woman was torn. She wanted to help, but she was afraid, as everyone was afraid.

"Please. I need somewhere safe to stay," Katy said softly. "I wouldn't ask if it were just for myself, but this baby in my belly is all I have left of Jacob. You remember what a good man he was and how much he did for you when you were sick while we stayed with you? Can you not repay his kindness by doing this for him now?"

Mrs. Statham did remember it. She'd had influenza while the Whites had been with her, and Katy had stayed by her side, bathing her with cold compresses until her fever had abated, while Jacob had taken over the running of the guesthouse and undertaken several repair jobs on the house. Mrs. Statham had been very sad to see them go once she was well. She had grown very fond of them both. "You were both very sweet and cared for me as if I were family. I've never forgotten it," she said cautiously.

"Please," Katy pleaded, her own eyes wide and beseeching, as she nervously played with her silver wedding ring, which was all that Jacob could afford back then. He'd offered to exchange it for a gold one once their circumstances had improved, but she hadn't wanted him to. It was the ring he had given her when they made their vows, and they had been all she ever needed from him. She didn't need gold to prove how much he cared for her.

"Oh, come in," the older woman said, standing aside and

letting Katy in. "You are right. I cannot turn you away after the kindness you showed me when I was sick. It is the very least I can do, to take you in now you are in need." She paused. "And I am sorry that you have lost dear Jacob. He was a fine young man."

# CHAPTER 3

*E*arly June 1878, Iron Creek, Minnesota

Garrett had begun to wonder if he would ever receive a response to his advertisement. It had been almost two months since he'd placed it, and though he knew well that the postal service often had delays, it had seemed a little too long—to his mind—for anyone to be interested. As the days and weeks without a reply had passed, he had put it to the back of his mind and accepted that even finding a mail-order bride might not be possible for a man like him.

He drank his morning coffee and slammed the cup down on the table, then grabbed his hat and headed out onto his narrow porch. He grabbed the bedroll and saddlebags he'd packed ready for his trip to the livestock market in Bemidji and headed for the barn. He'd be gone for at least three days and accommodation wasn't always available, and if he was successful, he would need to sleep out while he drove his herd of sheep home.

As he entered the barn, he was greeted by the nicker of his horse, Janus. The bay mustang nuzzled at Garrett's shoulder, seeking the affection that Garrett was more than happy to give. He'd found Janus when he'd first left the Ojibwe to make his way in the world. The young stallion had been badly hurt from a fight for dominance with the head of a local herd and had been left behind. Garrett nursed him back to health, then attempted to set him free—but Janus just kept coming back to him. Garrett had given up trying to let him loose after the fifth attempt, chose his name, and gentled him to a saddle and bridle. He'd proven to be the best mount Garrett had ever had.

Garrett led him out of his stall and brushed him down swiftly before fixing his tack. He tied his bedroll behind the saddle and the saddlebags to either side before he led Janus out of the barn and into the yard. He was about to mount up when the sound of hoofbeats on the narrow path to his left made him pause. It was rare that he had visitors—and they usually came from the direction of Red Lake, up the narrow path to the right of his cabin, where the Ojibwe made their home.

He turned to see Hank Wilson, the town's postmaster, riding toward him. "Hey, Hank," he called in greeting. "What can I do for you?"

"Nothing," Hank said with a grin. "But I have a letter for you." He dug into his saddlebag and pulled out a letter. "Right pretty handwriting." He winked at Garrett, who took the letter and tucked it into his back pocket. "You've not had many folks writing to you since you've been here. I'd have kept it in the office, but I guess I was curious as to who might be sending you such a letter."

"I'm sure I don't know," Garrett said. "I'll open it later. Right now, I'm off to market to buy myself some sheep." Hank Wilson was a nice enough man, but he was terribly nosey. His job as postmaster gave him unique access to knowledge that wasn't really any of his business, and Garrett didn't want to become one of his topics of gossip. Things were hard enough for him in Iron Creek as it was. Garrett wasn't much of a mixer, and his solitary ways had made him the subject of a lot of speculation.

"Well, I'll wish you good luck and be on my way, then," Hank said, obviously a little put out that Garrett hadn't opened the letter in front of him.

"Thanks for the delivery," Garrett said with a rare smile. "And don't go out of your way for me in the future. I can pick my mail up in town, as I've always done."

"Well, sure, if you say so," Hank said, clearly even more put out that he was going to get nothing from Garrett to tell the townsfolk. He reluctantly turned his horse's head and began back down the path to Iron Creek.

Garrett grinned and pulled out the letter. Hank was right; the handwriting was very pretty indeed. He ripped it open and began to read.

*Dear Gentleman of Minnesota,*

*I don't quite know how to begin such a letter as this, but I saw your advertisement and hope that I may be the kind of woman you are looking for. I think I should say this up front, but I am recently widowed and find myself quite alone in the world. It isn't a place I am happy to be, and do not wish for anyone to think I am seeking marriage too soon, that I did not care for my husband. I did. Very much. But this isn't a world where one can afford to mourn the dead for too long, and so I must look now to my future.*

*I worked in service before my marriage, was a chambermaid for a fine lady and gentleman in Richmond, Virginia. I am hardworking and would make you an excellent housekeeper. I hope that my bravery is evident, in that I am writing to you now, with the intention of starting a new life somewhere. It isn't the first time.*

*My parents did not approve of the man I married and cut me off. We left Richmond, the only home I'd ever known, so he could take up a position in New Orleans. We could have floundered, but we thrived. It was hard at times, and there were moments when I wished things could be different, but we continued onward, always looking forwards.*

*Now, without him, I must do the same. It will not be easy. I know that. And I know that it will be hard for me to let go of him and the love I bore him—though I know I must. No man wishes to be second best, but if you will be patient with me, I am sure that I will make you a fine wife. I work hard, and people tell me I have a good heart.*

*I will wait in Memphis for a reply, but not for long as they have the fever, too. I shall continue onward, to St. Louis and then to Chicago. Forgive me if it takes me some time to respond to your letters, should you reply, but I do not know where I will be staying after I leave Memphis so it is the only address I can give you with any confidence. The lady who owns the boarding house there will send on any correspondence if you do write.*

*Yours, most hopefully*

*Katy White*

She was certainly forthright. He doubted that such words would hold much sway with many men; they'd want honeyed words and would not want to hear of the love a woman bore another man. But Garrett appreciated her honesty. The truth mattered to him more than anything. He had been cheated too many times, by both those he loved and those he did not care for at all, and it was better to start from a point of clarity in his mind. Yet he was not sure that he should be taking advantage of a woman so clearly in desperate straits. He felt anger on her behalf that her family had disowned her. She should have been able to turn to them in her hour of need, not have to write to a complete stranger and hope that he might take her in.

He'd read in the newspapers about the yellow fever outbreak in the south. Too many people were falling sick, frightening numbers had died already, and people were fleeing for their lives. This young woman, so recently a widow, should not have to tie herself to a man in order to have somewhere to escape to. A loving family would surely be glad to step in, to help—as his own always did when he made a mess of things in his life. But he knew he was blessed to have been found and raised by Zaaga. She would never let any living thing flounder, and she had taught him to always look out for those who could not care for themselves.

He ran inside and grabbed some paper and a pen. He

quickly wrote a reply. It was short and to the point, but he hoped it was enough.

*Dear Mrs. White,*

*I am so grateful for your very honest letter. You have had much to deal with, and I cannot blame you for wanting to escape your current circumstances. It must be so frightening to be surrounded by death and disease as you have been.*

*Come to me here, in Iron Creek. I will arrange a position for you with one of the families in town. I am sure there will be at least one that will be glad of the help. If they will not put you up, I will also find you somewhere you can live, safely and in peace. There is no need for us to discuss marriage at this stage. We can get to know each other better once you are here. I think that, now, you need a friend more than you need a husband.*

*I have enclosed tickets for travel for you from Chicago to Minneapolis. I am unsure of where this might reach you or I would send tickets for you for the entire journey. I can also recommend that you take rooms at Mrs. Havermeier's boarding house in Chicago when you get that far. She is a very fine woman and will gladly take you in. I shall write to her as I write to you, telling her to expect your arrival. I shall meet you in Minneapolis.*

*Write to me once you get to Chicago, please. The drive from Iron Creek to Minneapolis is overland, and even with a fine carriage and regular changes of horses, it can take a week, so rest with Mrs. Havermeier until you hear from me that I am on my way. If you arrive in Minneapolis before me, I*

*recommend the Resting Place, a small hotel near the station.
The owner, Mr. Grayson, is a good friend of mine.*

*Yours, most sincerely*

*Garrett Harding*

Garrett looked back through the letter he'd just written. There was little in it to explain why he would be so generous, and nothing about himself at all, but he did not know how to write such things. The words would not come. He had never been one for sharing his thoughts and feelings. All he knew was that he would do all he could to help her, as the Ojibwe had done for him—taking him in when he needed it most. But he would not force her into a marriage to do so. He would have much rather enjoyed a lengthy courtship, by letter and perhaps with occasional visits, before making a decision to wed, anyway. There was much they would need to learn about each other. This would be better for them both.

True to his word, he also wrote a letter to Mrs. Havermeier before heading to Grand Marais for the livestock market. The thirty or so miles would give him time to reconsider whether or not to mail the letters he'd just written. If he did go through with it, it would be easier to post the letters in Grand Marais rather than have Hank speculate as to what was going on. Garrett didn't want to be the subject of endless gossip. He was a very private man, and until he knew what was happening, he didn't want anyone else poking their nose in.

The ride cross-country to Grand Marais was long, but a real pleasure. Garrett had always loved it, but this time, he barely noticed the lakes and rivers or the majestic snow-capped mountains in the distance. His mind was filled with the letters in his pocket and whether he should send them or not. Mrs. White seemed genuine enough. She'd been honest with him; at least he presumed she had. He would have thought that someone would have chosen more flattering words if they intended to exploit him. Mrs. White had been most forthright. She had told him her husband had only recently passed away, that she needed somewhere to run to—someone to run to. She probably didn't mind who it was, given her circumstances.

He couldn't bear the thought that someone less respectful than himself might have received a similar letter from her and might think to take advantage of a woman so clearly in need of a friend. Zaaga would not forgive him if he didn't do all he could to protect a woman so at risk, and he did not like to ever disappoint his mother. She would expect him to do what he could to help any stranger in need. He prayed that his letter would reach her before she agreed to join some other man who might not be so concerned for her welfare.

But by helping her, he was still no closer to a bride. If she decided she didn't like him, or he didn't like her well enough, he would be no closer to a match than he had been when he wrote that ridiculous advertisement. What if he never found anyone he could be himself with? Someone who would accept him as he was—confused, a little white, a little Ojibwe, and a lot alone. But that should not be Mrs. White's burden to bear.

As he rode into Bemidji after nightfall, he slipped the letters under the door of the postal office along with money to cover the postage. It wouldn't open until the morning, but Garrett knew that the postmaster would do what was necessary and send them onward when he opened up. Then he headed to the saloon. For once, he didn't stop at the bar to drink or take note of the poker game going on in the corner. He went straight up to his room and collapsed on the bed and wondered if he'd done the right thing in arranging to bring a stranger to Iron Creek without knowing anything about her. He could only pray that he had.

# CHAPTER 4

*L*ate June 1878, Memphis, Tennessee

Katy did not wish to remain long in Memphis. Yellow fever was raging there, just as out of control and just as deadly as it had been in New Orleans. She had to get away. Yet she had heard nothing from any of the men she had written to. Katy still had nowhere to go—no purpose to her flight. She stared out of the window at the unusually quiet streets and prayed that someone might come to the house with a letter for her soon. Mrs. Statham was not pushing her to go, but Katy knew she could not stay there much longer. Every day that passed, the older woman expressed regret that Katy would not be staying longer. She'd grown used to having the company, and the two women cared for each other as best they could amid all the chaos around them.

But despite her desire to be on her way, Katy realized how tired she was. She hadn't relaxed in months. All the stress and strain of nursing Jacob, of losing Jacob, and then having to think about what she might have to do to provide for their unborn child had taken a toll on her, and she simply slept for days. Katy barely knew how long she'd been there when Mrs. Statham knocked on her door gently one bright and sunny morning. "May I come in?" she asked cautiously.

"Of course," Katy called, pulling a robe over her slip as she tried to get out of the comfortable feather bed.

"Stay where you are," Mrs. Statham said as she entered with a tray. Katy smiled and settled back under the blankets.

The older woman placed the tray on Katy's lap. "I've brought you a treat. Some hot chocolate and a few pastries from the baker. He's French, and they are heavenly." Her blue eyes sparkled with pleasure. Katy took a bite of one of the perfectly glazed pastries and sighed. Rich with butter, flaky, and light, they were indeed spectacular. "He told me that in France, they dip them in the chocolate, but I've never dared try it."

Katy grinned and did so. It was pure heaven. The moistness added a whole different level of flavor and texture to the delicious feast. "That is fantastic. He's quite right," she declared and offered the elderly lady one of the pastries to try.

Tentatively, Mrs. Statham took one and delicately dunked a small piece into the hot chocolate. She took a bite, then closed her eyes and sighed happily. "I should have listened. He told me years ago, and I dismissed the idea." There was something almost wistful about the way she said it, and it made Katy wonder if there was more to this kind woman's relationship with the French baker than she was letting on.

"Is there anything else he may have suggested that you've dismissed?" Katy asked. Mrs. Statham blushed.

"Well, he's sent me flowers and asked me to go walking with him on many occasions. But I am too old and set in my ways to want a man now. It would be unseemly at my age."

"Who said that courting needed to lead to marriage and sharing your home? Can you not simply have a good friend whose company you enjoy?" Katy asked.

"It wouldn't be right," Mrs. Statham said primly, but Katy could see that she was tempted by such a thought.

"I often wonder why such things aren't seen to be proper and decent for women while men are permitted any leeway they desire," she mused. "Why shouldn't you enjoy someone's company? You are a respectable woman. He is a respectable man. There is nothing indecent about friendship, after all."

Mrs. Statham shrugged, and Katy wondered if the older woman might reconsider her strict rules and permit herself to welcome the attention of this man she so clearly liked and admired. Sadly, she doubted it. Older people seemed to be so bound by the rules they had grown up with and often struggled to realize that they were free to live their lives however they pleased. Mrs. Statham gave her a wry smile and left her alone with the rest of her breakfast.

Finally, after some weeks had passed, a letter arrived. It was short and gave her little information about the man who'd sent it, but his generosity was clear. He was not insisting upon marriage. He said he would help her, that he would find her a position and a home. And he had sent her the rail tickets she would need to travel from Chicago to Minneapolis, where he would meet her. She bit her lip as she re-read the letter. She did not know what to think. Should she take the risk that going to meet this man might bring? Was he what he seemed?

Katy did not know, so she hurried down the stairs and into the little parlor where Mrs. Statham spent her mornings and handed her the letter, hovering by the fireplace and waiting for her response. Mrs. Statham put on her spectacles and held the letter close to her face so she could read the gentleman's neat but tiny script. She sighed, tapped her fingers on the arm of her chair, and then looked up at Katy. "He's a man of few words, is he not?" she said with a smile.

"But are they words I can trust? What do you think?" Katy asked nervously.

Mrs. Statham shrugged. "How can we know?" she asked simply. "You are taking a gamble, whatever you choose to do, whether you travel on alone and try to make a life for yourself without a husband or jump at the first man to respond. But you need to learn more about him, somehow."

Katy knew she was right. There was little she could do to be certain of any outcome. She simply had to survive. Anything more than that could wait. This man claimed to offer her a new start. He wasn't insisting that she become his wife. He seemed to want to help her. And perhaps, if they continued to exchange letters as she traveled, she might learn more about him. She could make up her mind about whether to meet him once she reached Chicago.

"Will you send on any correspondence to me?" she asked Mrs. Statham. "I shall continue onward. I have little choice. Perhaps he might write to me again?"

"Of course, I shall," Mrs. Statham agreed. "And I can send you with a letter of introduction to my sister in St. Louis. She will give you a bed for a while if you need it, so any mail can catch up with you."

"Thank you," Katy said. She bent down and pressed a kiss on the older woman's cheek. Her skin was papery and smelled of violets from the soap she used, and lavender from her face powder. Mrs. Statham smiled at her and patted Katy's hand.

"You be careful," she warned. "Not all men are what they seem."

"I know that well enough," Katy said with a wry smile. "But I think I can tell a good one from a bad one—at least I hope so. I certainly got it right last time, though everyone told me Jacob was no good."

She returned to her room and sat on the bed, cross-legged, to write to Mr. Harding. It took her three attempts, but eventually, she had something she felt she could send him.

*Dear Mr. Harding,*

*Thank you kindly for your letter, the tickets, and your generous offer to help me to settle in Iron Creek. I cannot tell you what it means to me to have such assistance. It has been a very difficult time, following the loss of my husband and everything I have known. To receive such kindness from a stranger is surprising and gratefully received. I can assure you that once I am settled, I intend to repay you for the tickets and any costs you might incur on my behalf.*

*I must confess, I am glad that you made no mention of marriage as a condition of such generosity. I am well aware that I responded to a matrimonial advertisement, but I have not yet had time to fully mourn my dear husband, Jacob, and though I am prepared to do what is necessary, I am glad that you do not deem a hasty wedding to be one of those things. I would rather we get to know each other a little better before we make such a life-changing decision.*

*So, to commence our acquaintanceship, I will begin. My name is Katherine, though everyone calls me Katy. I was born on board the ship that brought my parents from England to America, and they chose to settle in Richmond, Virginia. My father was a carpenter by trade, and he soon built himself a reputation as the finest maker of windows and doors in the city. We lived a comfortable enough life—not rich, but certainly not too poor. We had enough for a few small luxuries and for my education.*

*When I turned sixteen, I met Jacob White. He was dashing and handsome, just a few years older than me at nineteen, newly arrived in the city from Boston. He flattered me and courted me, and all my friends were jealous of the attention he paid me. He was apprenticed to a blacksmith and would have a fine future. Yet my family did not approve of him. I still do not know why. But I would not give him up, and when I turned seventeen, he asked me to marry him and go with him, as he had gained employment on a paddle steamer in New Orleans.*

*My parents never spoke to me again, though I wrote often. I hoped every time that Mam might one day reply, even if Pa could not forgive me, but I heard nothing and so had to accept, eventually, that I was alone in this world but for Jacob. We created a good life for ourselves. Jacob was happier working on the river than he had been as an apprentice, and he was promoted swiftly. We had a nice little home, near the French Quarter, and we were as happy as we could be.*

*And then, yellow fever struck the city. Jacob, being in contact with many men, women, and children on the steamers, as they came into the city from the port, did all he could to stay safe and to keep me safe, but eventually, he succumbed to the disease. I am not sure how I did not contract it, but somehow, I did not, despite nursing him through every minute of his illness. He passed away, and I knew I had to get away from the city before I, too, got ill.*

*And so, I wrote to you. And you have responded with a kindness I did not expect from a stranger. I thank you for that.*

*I should perhaps speak a little of my interests, as I am not just a widow. I love to read. I love Dickens and Wilkie Collins and have recently discovered the fantastical works of Jules Verne. They have such imaginations, such clever ways of expressing themselves. I should love to write so well.*

*Before I was married, I was obsessed with horses. My pa had a couple of horses for his cart, and he gave me a chestnut pony for my twelfth birthday. I could always be found in the stables, grooming them all and keeping their stalls and tack clean as a button. I should very much like to ride regularly again. We could not afford to keep a horse in New Orleans.*

*I do so hope you will reply to me. I have included the address of the boarding house I will stay at in St. Louis and will take your advice and stay at Mrs. Havermeier's in Chicago, so hopefully, if you write to me at either of them, the letters should reach me.*

*Thank you again. I look forward to meeting you in person.*

*Yours, most gratefully*
*Mrs. Katy White*

Once she had given the letter to Mrs. Statham to post, Katy packed her bags and set out that very afternoon. She was lucky to get a place on the train to St. Louis, and quickly settled herself into her seat and pulled out a book she'd brought with her for the journey. She loved to read, though books were expensive, and she could rarely afford new ones. This particular book, *A Tale of Two Cities* by Charles Dickens, she had read several times, but she still loved it. She loved all of Dickens' stories, but this was her favorite. It was set in London and Paris, and Katy liked to imagine herself in both cities, living a different life. Though she did not wish to have the experiences of Dr. Mannette in the Bastille.

# CHAPTER 5

*E*arly July 1878, St. Louis, Missouri

The train flew across the miles, covering the distance it would have taken weeks to cover by wagon in only a few days. Katy barely noticed the changes in scenery outside the window of the fast-moving steam train, so engrossed was she in her book, but from time to time, the hard bench reminded her that she was not at home in her favorite armchair, and she would look up for a few moments and fidget just enough to get comfortable on her cushion once more. Each time she did so, she saw new people in the carriage and gaps on the benches where those who had got off the train no longer sat.

She couldn't help noticing that everyone on board looked concerned, scared of the disease sweeping the south, no doubt, and they all kept to themselves, not wishing to so much as talk above a whisper, much less bump into someone else in the aisles. Nobody wanted contact with anyone they did not know. It created a brooding and tense atmosphere, which was easier to escape from in her book than pay attention to by glancing around too often. Nobody paid her much mind and Katy was happy to be so unnoticed.

But being in a cramped carriage with so many strangers was not an enjoyable experience, and Katy was glad to disembark in St. Louis and rest there for a while. Yellow fever had not struck this city as hard as it had its more southerly neighbors.

Mrs. Statham's sister welcomed her warmly, fed her with hearty stews and oatmeal with honey, and was quite happy for her to stay as long as she liked, though Katy was determined not to stay too long. She waited anxiously each day for the mail to arrive and was disappointed when nothing was delivered for her.

Katy wanted to get to Chicago as soon as she could. St. Louis still felt too close to the disease she was fleeing from, so she determined to give Mr. Harding only a couple of weeks to respond to her last letter. If he did not do so, she would just have to hope that he would write to her care of Mrs. Havermeier in Chicago instead. She had come this far, and she could not turn back now. If she ended up stranded in Chicago, at least it was a busy city where she would most likely be able to find work and a room.

She passed the time helping Miss Ginsberg around the house as much as she could. The elderly lady was frailer than her younger sister but just as determined. She lived life on her own terms. Over supper one night, Katy told her about the

French baker that had been trying to court Mrs. Statham and she laughed. "Dear Blanche was always so prissy," she said. "Never took a chance. She let Papa marry her off to Harold Statham, and the silly ninny thought herself in love. The man was a rummy. It was the best thing that happened to Blanche when he upped and died, leaving her that house."

"I got the impression she had a happy marriage," Katy said, surprised at such a revelation.

"Far from it. Blanche wanted children; Harold did not. She wished to live here in St. Louis, nearer to me, and he refused. He said it was because there was more opportunity in Memphis, but really, he just wanted to isolate her from her family. He was a nasty piece of work, and she's been happier since he's been dead, I can tell you."

"Then why does she resist the possibility of remarrying?" Katy pondered aloud. "It seemed quite clear that she has feelings for the French baker."

"Perhaps she fears being trapped again, though she'd never admit it," Miss Ginsberg said as she passed Katy a platter of roast beef. Katy took two slices and helped herself to vegetables from the tureen in the center of the table. "I keep telling her that she need not fear that," Miss Ginsberg went on. "But I may have also overpraised the life of a single woman to her when Harold passed away."

"What do you mean?"

Miss Ginsberg chuckled. "Well, I was always a bit untraditional. I managed to avoid my father's marital machinations and took a position as a governess in a house here in St Louis. I rented rooms away from the household I worked in, and in private I had my affairs and lived life on my own terms. I don't think anyone approved. My parents virtually disowned me and barely spoke to me, even when they invited me to share Christmas with them."

"I'm sorry. I know how hard it is to be cast adrift," Katy empathized.

"When the children I cared for were grown, I was too old to consider marriage and a family of my own. I used my savings to purchase this little house, and I started to let out the rooms. I met so many wonderful people, and I talked about how happy I was to Blanche. I think she thought she would be as happy as me, but she and I are very different people. Perhaps I should write to her and tell her to take her chances while she still can."

Katy smiled. She hoped that Mrs. Statham would consider her talented baker for a chance at the love that had so clearly passed her by in her first marriage, if Miss Ginsberg's account was correct, and Katy had no reason to doubt this gregarious and feisty old woman. As the pair continued their meal, the conversation ranged from Katy's plans for the future to Miss Ginsberg's favorite lover—an actor called Merrill Davison— who had promised her the world, only for his wife to arrive at the theater one night, catching Miss Ginsberg and the actor *in flagrante*. She laughed about it, but Katy wondered if she had been so calm about it then. Personally, she would have been mortified.

As they finished, Miss Ginsberg stood up, cleared some of the dishes, and moved to the door. She glanced at the mantel briefly, then shook her head. "Oh my, I'd forget my own head these days, were it not pinned on there so tightly," she said, giving Katy an apologetic look. "There is a letter there for you, my dear girl. It came this morning." She pointed to the mantelpiece, where a letter was propped up against the clock.

Katy hurried to fetch it "Thank you," she said. She opened the letter immediately and saw the return address and now-familiar handwriting. She smiled and opened it as the older woman left the room.

*Dear Mrs. White,*

*Thank you for your letter, and for introducing yourself more thoroughly to me. I hope I will do a better job in telling you more about myself than I did in my last missive.*

*I was delighted to find that you once enjoyed horseback riding. Being able to ride will be of great benefit as there are no railways nearby, and travel by cart, wagon, and on horseback are the only options—though there is talk of extending the railways, so in time we may see a station in Bemidji or even in the small town of Iron Creek.*

*I live on the outskirts of the town, on a small lake in the hills, and have just purchased a herd of sheep. The land up here isn't suitable for much, but they seem to like it. It can be a little lonely in these parts, but like you, I enjoy reading. I am also an avid reader of Mr. Dickens but I personally prefer David Copperfield to A Tale of Two Cities.*

*I was raised by the local Chippewa tribe, so I came to reading a little late, but I like to think I have made up for it since. My adoptive mother, Zaagaasikwe, always says that I was a gift from the ancestors, but I ended up in her path due to a dreadful accident that killed both my parents. It has been strange to grow up not ever feeling a full member of the community I grew up in or the one I was born into.*

*I started out as a trapper and then became a trader. My connections with the Ojibwe (just one name the Chippewa give to themselves) made me a useful go-between. I'd act on behalf of the tribe and deal with the white men, as they thought me one of them. I used the connections I had to build enough wealth to purchase my own bit of land, so I could raise my sheep and work where I best belong.*

*So, you will not be alone in trying to learn how to live in a strange new world. Perhaps we can help each other to settle and find out what is next for us as we travel through life?*

*I do hope my telling you this does not concern you. I know many would be afraid of a man who was raised by Indians, but I can assure you my mother raised me to be a good man, to respect women, and to take care of those I care about. I will do no less for you than I do for her. She is my world—and is wise and strong in every way. I sometimes wish I had even half of her courage, fortitude, and certainty.*

*I look forward to our meeting and hope that you will write to me again soon.*

*Yours, most humbly*

*Garrett Harding*

Katy was touched deeply by how much he had chosen to share with her. He had told her things that many men would not have, and he did not need to speak of his upbringing, nor of his affection and admiration for his adoptive mother, yet he had done so. It spoke volumes to Katy about his decency. She cared little if he had been raised by the Chippewa, or by wolves. She'd worked for those who considered themselves among the elite of society in Richmond, and from time to time in New Orleans when money had been tight. She knew all too well that having wealth and power did not necessarily make someone a good human being.

Of course, she'd read the newspapers and all their lurid tales about the savagery of the native tribes, but she'd never experienced it herself. She'd lived in places where, for the most part, such peoples had been moved from or already wiped out long before she and her family had arrived. She knew that most women would be scared silly by his revelation. But to her, it was something new to learn about. How different had his childhood been from hers? And why did he now feel so apart from both his adopted people and those whose blood he shared? It must be very hard to feel that you belonged nowhere.

But it was his words about his mother that made Katy sure that he was a good man. Mr. Harding was not afraid of a strong woman. He was proud of his mother, and he appreciated her and wished to emulate *her*—not some other man. It was as reassuring as it was unusual. Katy could not wait to meet such a man. Perhaps he would be the kind to let a woman be herself and follow her own path. She certainly hoped so because, as she was learning from Mrs. Statham and Miss Ginsberg, a woman alone did not need to accept that she had to take another husband. She could forge her own path.

After dessert had been eaten and the dishes had been washed and put away, Katy went up to her room and lay on her bed, staring up at the whitewashed ceiling. She caressed her belly, wondering for a moment if she might be having a son or a daughter. It didn't matter to her. She just wanted to see the child safely into the world. She pondered whether to tell Mr. Harding before she arrived, or whether it was the kind of news that would be better imparted in person. He had been honest with her about his upbringing. Should she not be honest with him about her unborn child?

The thought had played on her mind ever since she'd written to him and received his first letter, but still, she had no answer. But if she was not intending to wed him, did it matter? Could she find a way to earn enough money to support herself and the child? It was all well and good for a spinster with no children like Miss Ginsberg to find a way to live on her own terms, but Katy would soon be a mother. Whether she liked it or not, people did not think a woman alone was capable of bringing up a child—especially if that child was a son.

# CHAPTER 6

*L*ate July 1878, Iron Creek, Minnesota

A group of young boys, none of them older than seven years of age, were playing in the creek when Garrett stopped to let Janus take a drink. They splashed and chased one another loudly. Garrett smiled with a hint of sadness. They were around the age that Ano would have been, had he survived. Perhaps Ano would have been friends with them, playing in the cold water to cool down in the warm summer sun. Perhaps Garrett would never have moved to Iron Creek, and might have returned to the tribe if he'd lived? It hurt Garrett sometimes to think of what he'd lost, so he tried his best not to think about it. But every now and again, scenes such as this brought it back to him.

He didn't like to think of his lost love, Oma. It hurt too much to think about how things had turned out, so he tried to do all he could to banish those thoughts when they arose, inevitably as they did, from time to time. She had been so perfect, so calm, and so sweet. She had bravely followed him when he left home to explore the part of himself that he knew nothing about, though she must have known how hard that would be for her—for them both. She had never once scolded him for forcing her into a life where she could never possibly fit in.

He certainly didn't like to think of the abuse she had faced because of that choice, or how hard it had been for them both to face down the criticism, the taunts, and sometimes the outright violence they had faced as a couple. It seemed to him that the people he was born of had been unable to tolerate such an abomination in their eyes, and they still were unable, sadly. So, though they had barely reconciled after a period where he had been far away for many months, he'd made her stay with Zaaga when they found out that she was pregnant. If the white men were unhappy about his choice to wed an Ojibwe, heaven alone knew how they would react to the thought of such a couple having children.

But it wasn't just that. He'd wanted her to have the best of care and to be safe with her family and people who loved and cared about her. He knew that there would always be someone on hand to take care of Oma if she stayed with the tribe. He had wanted their child to know from the start the place it would always be safe, wanted, and loved. That had been before he knew the truth, of course. But it hadn't been enough. His beloved wife had died giving birth to little Ano, and Garrett's sweet boy had died just a few days after his naming.

And he hadn't been there.

Garrett could never forgive himself for that. He had made the last years of Oma's life a living hell, dragging her away from her home and family, subjecting her to taunts and attacks, just for the sin of loving him. Then he'd sent her away because he couldn't bear to see how unhappy she was. And when she'd needed him most, he had been drowning his sorrows in a saloon while claiming he was transacting important business. That business had been an important poker game that cost him the land he'd purchased to make a home for himself and Oma. He had literally lost everything and still hadn't learned his lesson.

And then he had learned the truth—that Ano might not even have been his. Dibikad had come to him after Oma's burial rites and confessed. Garrett had been inconsolable, but it was a secret he could not talk about. After Oma and Ano's deaths, Garrett had become too afraid to return home. Not only was it too hard for him to face the places he had once walked with his wife in happier times, but he had been unable to face Dibikad or his own family. He carried so much guilt, even though Oma had been drawn to his oldest friend in his absence.

And he had feared the righteous anger of Oma's kin. They felt very strongly that he was the reason she'd been so unhappy, and that he was the reason she was no longer walking this earth. He couldn't face them, so he'd stayed away, withdrawing into himself more and more with each passing day. He had buried himself in drink, continued to gamble, and even lost Janus in a card game near Duluth. But his ever-faithful mount wouldn't let anyone else ride him; he kicked down the gates when his new owner tried to pen him and found his way home. He always came back to Garrett. No matter what.

He thought about the most recent letter he'd received from Mrs. White. It sounded as though she had not enjoyed the easiest of lives, either. Yet she was not afraid to be honest with him about it. She had told him of her lost husband and the loss of her family. He wondered if he should tell her more about his past, but he knew he could not yet talk about most of it. It was still too raw, too painful—and it had been the reason that even when he'd tried to put his drinking and gambling behind him, he'd kept his distance from both the Ojibwe and the townsfolk in Iron Creek. He couldn't bear their condemnation —or worse, their pity.

Perhaps it was for the best that nobody who truly longed for marriage had replied to his advertisement. He knew now he was not ready to face the potential for pain that allowing someone so close would create. He would do all he could to help Mrs. White rebuild her life. She deserved a new start, and he would be the friend she needed. He couldn't allow himself to feel anything more than that. She'd had enough heartbreak. He resolved not to bring her anymore.

Reaching for Janus' reins, he led the horse into Iron Creek and hitched him up outside the general store. He went inside, tipped his hat to the ladies, and gave a tight smile to the men. A few greeted him, but mostly he was left to his own devices. When it was his turn at the counter, Judd Barclay gave him a hearty handshake. "Good to see you, Harding," he boomed. "I've got your order out back. You got your cart with you?"

"Not now. I'll stop by later, if that's alright with you?" he said, handing over a handful of dollar bills to pay his account. "I'm just on Janus."

"I'm passing by your way later, so I can drop it by if you'd like," Judd said generously.

"Nobody passes by my way," Garrett said with a laugh. "I live in the middle of nowhere. There's nobody beyond my place but the Ojibwe."

Judd gave a wry smile. "I was trying to..." he tailed off, not entirely sure what he'd been trying to do.

"Make me feel like everyone else?" Garrett said.

"I guess. It's the sort of thing I'd do for anyone in town. I always feel you miss out and have to do things twice as hard just because you're out so far."

"I chose my spot, Judd," Garrett said gently. "There's no need to fret on my behalf, my friend."

"I know. You can take care of yourself. You like being all alone out there. I've heard it all before. But the offer's there."

"And if you'll agree to have potluck, then you'd be most welcome to stop by with my order. You'll need to add some beer to it, though. Perhaps even a bottle of whiskey."

"Now that's an offer I can't refuse. I've never had a bad meal at your shack in all your time there. I'll be with you around seven, after I close up here," Judd said enthusiastically.

Garrett smiled and left the store. Judd was a good man, and the two were similar in many ways. Both had lost their wives in childbirth, though Judd's boy was one of the lads that Garrett had seen down at the creek earlier. Garrett wondered if Judd had ever considered remarrying. He'd never dared to ask, and probably never would. Such a thing was a man's own private concern.

He unhitched Janus and wandered along Main Street, toward the smithy. Alec Jenks was another lone man in a town filled with happily married men. As Garrett turned into the yard, Alec was bent over the fire, a horseshoe in the tongs he was wielding in his giant hands. Alec towered over every man Garrett had ever known. He had the strength of four men, yet was also one of the kindest men Garrett had ever known. The man was gentle and sweet, and Garrett was certain he'd make a good husband if he ever left his forge long enough to meet someone.

"Good day to you, Alec," Garrett called. "You got a home for that?" he nodded toward the horseshoe that Alec was now hammering out on the anvil.

"No, just preparing some ahead of time," Alec said.

"Good, because Janus needs new shoes," Garrett said, tying Janus up away from the fire.

Alec put the horseshoe down and moved toward Janus. He ran his hand down the horse's neck, down his back, and down his back leg. Janus patiently lifted his hoof. It always surprised Garrett how cooperative the temperamental horse could be for Alec. He had certainly never behaved that way for anyone else but Garrett. Within just a few moments, Alec had checked all four hooves and started to remove the shoes. Janus barely moved a muscle throughout, even when Alec shaped the shoes, pressed them to his hooves, and started hammering them into place.

Janus rewarded the gentle blacksmith with a tender nuzzle

at his neck, and Alec rubbed his nose and patted his neck affectionately. "I know, you're the best of horses," he said softly.

"You truly have a gift," Garrett said. "I've had smiths threaten to run me out of town when I've taken him to be shod in the past."

"Janus? He's good as gold," Alec said, still petting the horse.

"For me, for you—but for nobody else," Garrett said. "How much do I owe you?"

Alec gave him his price, and Garrett paid him and mounted Janus. He rode back out onto Main Street and turned toward home. Hank Wilson must have seen him riding by the postal office and came running out into the street. "I've got another letter for you, Garrett," he said excitedly. "Same handwriting as the last one."

"Not that it's any of your business," Garrett said drily. "But thank you." He took the letter from Hank's outstretched hand and tucked it in his pocket, then continued to ride home.

Back at the shack, he fixed a rich venison stew and set it to cook over a fire he lit outside the cabin and put some potatoes in the embers to bake in their skins. He pulled a couple of chairs out of the shack, ready for Judd's arrival, then sat down and pulled out the letter. He smiled at Mrs. White's handwriting. In comparison to his own tiny, neat handwriting, hers was a flowery, extravagant scrawl. He imagined the abandon she wrote with and wondered if she lived the rest of her life that way.

*Dear Mr. Harding,*

*Thank you for your letter. It reached me in St. Louis just before I left. When you receive this, I will hopefully have just arrived in Chicago and will be making plans to travel onward to Minneapolis. I do so hope you will be able to meet me there.*

*The journey has been both tedious and fascinating in equal measure. I have had plenty of time to read, and the scenery has been quite spectacular at times, but I can tell you, I shall be glad not to travel anywhere by railway ever again. The benches are too uncomfortable for such a long trip as this, even with a trusty cushion to ease my pain!*

*I was honored by the frankness of your letter. Growing up among the Ojibwe must have been very different from my more conventional upbringing. I do hope that someday you will care to share more about it with me. All I know of the native tribes is that my kind, our kind, have generally treated them very badly yet look upon such behavior as somehow heroic.*

*I don't know about you, but I think man's penchant to wage war against anyone and anything he doesn't understand is one of his least attractive traits. I would like to think that perhaps someday people will learn to live with one another in peace, though I fear it may be a foolish dream on my part.*

*I thought I should perhaps tell you of the things that I am capable of doing in order for you to help me to find a position, as you suggested. As I think I said in an earlier letter, I was in service previously, so I know how to run a household. My parents also ensured I had an excellent education, so I could perhaps take on a position as a governess, or even a school-teacher, should such things be required in Iron Creek. I also took the odd shift in the local general store in New Orleans when money was hard to find and they needed help. I learn quickly and am not concerned about what I might have to do. I have no airs and graces.*

*Can you tell me more about your home? I know you are in the part of the country near Lake Superior. I've seen pictures of the lake but know little of the region. If you could perhaps tell me why you choose to remain there, to make it your home. I am so looking forward to seeing it—and you.*

*Yours hopefully*

*Mrs. Katy White*

# CHAPTER 7

*E*arly August 1878, Chicago, Illinois

The journey had grown more tedious as the miles passed. Katy longed to reach her destination, yet it seemed to her that she might not ever reach Chicago. She had read her book and now, with little to entertain herself with, she had nothing but her fears and worries to keep her company. There were so many thoughts she did not wish to think, yet they seemed to be all that played on her mind.

She tried not to remember the last time she'd undertaken such a long journey, the bittersweet time when she and Jacob had headed from Richmond to New Orleans. Jacob had done all he could to ensure that the journey was as fun as possible. They had been newlyweds, so young and so sure they were right to take the chance for a different life—despite her parents' misgivings. Their love would overcome all hurdles, and they had been so determined to prove everyone wrong.

Of course, Katy had been sad that her parents had not attended her wedding, but she had convinced herself that it was of little matter. She and Jacob had each other and would face whatever was ahead together. It had been a lesson hard-learned, but Katy had come to realize that her parents were in part right—love alone was not enough. She'd missed her family every single day she had been apart from them. If they had only written, even once a year, on Christmas or her birthday perhaps, it might have been easier to bear, but the separation from them only grew harder with time, never easier as she'd so naively hoped.

When the train finally pulled into the station in Chicago, Katy wished with all her heart that it would be the last time she would ever see a railway station, though she knew she still had a long way to go if Mr. Harding was as good as his word and had indeed sent the tickets for her onward passage to Minneapolis.

She made her way to the boarding house he had recommended and was welcomed warmly by Mrs. Havermeier, who was indeed obviously very fond of Mr. Harding. The kindly widow spoke gushingly of the young man who had stayed with her some years before, and how delighted she was that he was now settled and content after the terrible tragedies he had faced so young. "He was in bits; I can tell you," she said, with concern in her eyes. "I am glad he's settled now. I feared he'd never find his place. And that he's been writing with a pretty thing like you—that gives me hope." She winked at Katy, who blushed furiously at the unexpected compliment.

"From his letters, he seems content enough there," Katy

said cautiously. She didn't dare to ask for more details about the bad things this friendly lady had mentioned—especially as the older woman talked to her of Mr. Harding's past troubles as if she must already know of them. She was too ashamed to admit that she barely knew the man's present, much less anything from his past, though it didn't stop her wondering what had happened. It must have been terrible since Mrs. Havermeier spoke now of it with such anguish in her kindly blue eyes.

"Now, I've put you in the front bedroom," Mrs. Havermeier said, showing Katy up the steep oak staircase onto a narrow landing. "It's the most comfortable. You can call down for hot water at any time, and Maisie will fetch it up for you." She gave Katy a gentle pat on the arm and opened a door. It opened onto a spacious room. It had whitewashed walls and was clean and bright. A large, metal-framed bed with a feather mattress dominated the space, but there was also room for a large armoire and a sizable chest of drawers to match it.

"Thank you, it is wonderful," Katy said as she went inside. The high ceiling and the large windows made the room feel airy and bright. She traced her finger over the rim of the porcelain ewer on the washstand and smiled at the obvious comfort of the overstuffed armchair in the window. "I shall never wish to leave."

"You'd be most welcome, but I know that Mr. Harding will be glad to know you've arrived safely. He was most concerned for your comfort when he told me you were coming. I shall write to him now to let him know you've arrived safely."

"Thank you, but I am happy to do so if you could perhaps fetch me some paper and a pen and ink?"

The older woman smiled. "Of course, you will want to write yourself," she said, shaking her head as if she had been silly to suggest anything otherwise. "But I'm sure you'll want to freshen up before you do anything. I shall be back shortly. I left his letter for you on the mantel, there." She nodded toward the fireplace and a small cream envelope Katy hadn't noticed before. She moved to fetch the letter as Mrs. Havermeier left the room. She broke the seal and opened it.

*Dear Mrs. White,*

*I do so hope that this finds you well. I know from personal experience how tedious it can be crossing the country, so do not envy you the journey. But now that you are nearly done, should you wish to remain with Mrs. Havermeier for any period of time in order to rest and recuperate after your journey so far, I have told her to send the bills to me here in Iron Creek.*

*The tickets you will need for the next part of your journey can be collected from the station in Chicago once you arrive. Mrs. Havermeier has her orders! She will arrange for any date you prefer. I do understand if you take your time, but please know that I would like to get you here as soon as possible so I can put my mind at rest that you are safe. It is a dangerous business, traveling on the railways in this part of the world. Please, do take care.*

*I have arranged for you to take up a position in town here and hope it will suit you. Mr. and Mrs. Jellicoe have just had twin boys. They are sweet as pie, but Mrs. Jellicoe is finding it hard managing them both, so could use some help with them and keeping the house spick and span. I hope it is the kind of position that will suit you. Mr. Jellicoe runs the local newspaper, so he is busy and works long hours. Both are kind, God-fearing folk that attend church in town every Sunday. In truth, without Mr. Jellicoe's efforts, there would be no church in Iron Creek. It was his hard work that got it built and raised the money to pay a minister.*

*As to why I chose to stay here, I am unsure, if I am truthful with you, and I hope to always be that. I was raised near here, and I think there is something to be said for such a thing. A part of me will always belong to this place. I think that had I been raised differently that might not be so true—the white men I know don't seem to have the same connection to a place that I and my Ojibwe brethren do. But I think it may also be because there is so much space. So much sky. So much land. I cannot imagine this part of the world ever being as busy as Chicago, or New York, or any of the other places on the east coast of the country. I enjoy the peace, the ability to spend days, sometimes, without ever seeing another soul.*

*That said, it can often be very lonely. And so, I chose a place close enough to a small town where I know everyone's name and they know me but is far enough away that they don't bother me all the time and get in my business when I wish to be left alone. My home is less than half a day's ride from my mother and the tribe, so I am close to her and can see her when I wish, though I do not return there as often as I should. Like me, my home straddles the two worlds I walk in, a midpoint one might say between the two.*

*I cannot wait to show you the lakes and rivers, the mountains and the animals and birds of this beautiful place. I do not wish to do so without your permission, but there is a mare I think might suit you well for sale in Grand Marais. I have convinced the owner to give me time to discuss it with you, but he will need an answer soon. She is a gray and has been trained as a lady's mount, so is used to a side-saddle. If you would prefer to wait, and choose a mount for yourself, I will understand; it is a most personal matter.*

*I look forward to our imminent meeting. It will not be long now.*

*Yours most impatiently,*

*Garrett Harding*

His words made Katy smile even more. He was making plans for her arrival. It showed he was thinking of her, even though he'd yet to meet her. And the way he spoke of his home as if it were almost a part of himself was something she had never experienced firsthand. She had never known the pull he spoke of for any place. She had been as happy in Richmond as she had been in New Orleans, and she could have happily remained in either Memphis or St. Louis, and Mrs. Havermeier's would make as good a home as any of those she had known before.

She began to unpack her things, then caught sight of her image in the cheval glass by the armoire. She had filled out considerably since she'd left New Orleans. There, she'd resembled a ghost with her pale skin and rapidly thinning body. All the good food prepared for her so generously by the kind women she had stayed with on this journey had helped her cheeks to color and plump out, but it was the burgeoning swell of her belly that was really starting to become a problem. She would only be able to bind it for so long, and though she could let out the waist of her gowns and even wear dresses that might hide it for a little longer, it was going to become more and more obvious with each passing day. If her calculations were correct, she did not have much time available to her before her predicament would be common knowledge, as she must already be close to four months along.

Yet it felt wrong to tell Mr. Harding of it by letter. She had grown to care for him, and such news should be delivered in person. That meant that even if she wished to stay in Chicago for a time, she could not afford to. She had to be settled soon so that when her pregnancy became news, nobody would turn her away for it. Katy knew how hard it could be to find a position with a child; few employers would take on a woman due to have one, much less once it was born. And she could not imagine that many men would truly be happy to take on another man's child—no matter how good and kind they might seem to be.

Mrs. Havermeier returned with a clean bath sheet over her arm and pails of hot water in each hand. "I was just going to bring up some water for the washstand, but then I thought you might like a soak in the tub," she said kindly. "I know I always feel so dirty whenever I have to travel on the railway." Behind her, a handsome young lad of no more than fifteen followed with a copper tub. He set it down beside the fire and beat a hasty retreat as Maisie appeared with more hot water.

Katy smiled at them as they filled the tub, then Maisie

went to the washstand and pulled open the little drawer beneath the bowl. She took out a small wooden box and sprinkled a good handful of the contents into the copper tub. A waft of lavender and roses filled the air. "Enjoy your bath, Miss," Maisie said, then disappeared on silent feet.

"I'll have paper and pen ready for you in the parlor when you're freshened up a little," Mrs. Havermeier said, giving Katy's arm a squeeze. "You just rest for a bit. The mail coach doesn't leave until tomorrow morning for Minnesota, so there's plenty of time."

"Thank you," Katy said gratefully, waiting for the older woman to leave her alone. She closed the door and turned the key in the lock before she stripped her clothes and sank into the hot water gratefully. She could feel the tensions of the miles and miles of travel ease from her body, though her fears for her future and that of her child did not dissolve so easily. She cradled her rapidly growing belly. "Will he mind that I have not told him of you? Should I write and tell him now or is it better to wait and tell him when we meet?" she asked the child inside. "Will he be happy that you are part of the package? Or will he hate me for not telling him sooner?"

# CHAPTER 8

*L*ate August 1878, Iron Creek, Minnesota

Another letter was waiting at the postal office when Garrett arrived in Iron Creek to fetch his groceries. When he saw the handwriting and that it had come from Chicago, he smiled. She was nearly here. He would never have thought it possible to become so very attached to someone he'd never met in person, yet the woman he'd encountered through letters alone was in many ways more real to him than anyone else he knew. He tucked the letter into his pocket, not wanting Hank to speculate as to its content, and went on his way with a tip of his hat.

Garrett went down to the creek and settled himself on a rock, letting Janus graze peacefully down at the water's edge. It was a beautiful day, with just enough breeze to make the warm summer sun pleasant. For a moment, he stared at the water as it trickled by, the water level low from all the fine weather they'd had recently, then tipped his hat back and took Mrs. White's letter out of his pocket.

*Dear Mr. Harding,*

*I cannot tell you how grateful I am that you have found me such a perfect position. I adore children and would be glad to be of help to Mrs. Jellicoe. If they are as nice as you say, I shall be most content with them, I am sure. I truly never expected to receive such kindness from a stranger and fear I may spend the rest of my days trying to find ways to thank you for it!*

*However, though I am grateful for your looking for a suit-able mount for me, and though I know a horse will probably be essential in such a place as you describe in your letters, I could not possibly accept a horse as a gift. So, though I would be delighted to possess what sounds like an ideal horse, I cannot afford it right now so fear I must decline for the time being. I shall just have to hope that a suitable animal can be found once I am in a position to buy one and pay for its upkeep. I know all too well just how much that can be.*

*Your home sounds quite captivating, and it is clear you love it very much. I have never truly felt that way about any place. My affection has always been reserved for people, rather than the spot I find myself in—though Richmond was nice enough and New Orleans was exciting and new. It must be nice to know where you belong, even if you are not entirely certain about who you belong with.*

*I miss my parents so much. I have never said this to anyone, not even to my late husband, but it has never stopped hurting that they cast me aside so easily. I had never thought their love was so conditional upon my doing as they wished—and only as they wished. They encouraged me to learn and to be the best person I could be, to have dreams, and to pursue them. Then it felt as though they punished me for doing as they said they wanted me to do. I doubt I will ever truly be reconciled to that notion. Should I ever be blessed with a child, I should wish them to follow their heart—as long as their head had considered the consequences as well!*

*I am keen to get my travels complete, so I hope that I will hear from you soon, to tell me you are on your way to meet me in Minneapolis. I look forward to that day with great anticipation. I feel that we have become good friends as we write back and forth and am glad of that, indeed. I am so tempted to get on the next train I can but will heed your words and wait for your response to this letter as patiently as I am able.*

*Yours in anticipation,*

*Mrs. Katy White*

He wasn't surprised that there were limits to what she might expect. She did not seem overly proud, but she possessed an independent nature. He would buy the mare anyway, he decided. She would make a fine addition to his own one-horse stable, and it would mean that Mrs. White could ride whenever she liked without having to rely upon the mounts in the public stable.

He was surprised at just how much she had chosen to confide in him. He knew he had told her things that nobody knew, except perhaps Zaaga, who was kind enough to pretend that she did not know them, but like Mrs. White, he had not expected such a close friendship to grow between them during their short correspondence. He was glad she felt that way, too. It gave him hope that there may be a chance of romance once she arrived.

He checked the date on the letter and nodded his head as he worked out how long it might take Mrs. White to reach Minneapolis. He knew well enough that even with the fastest of horses and regular changes along the route, it might take him a week to get there. And he would need to get someone to watch over his sheep while he was gone. He mounted Janus and raced back into town. He stopped at the forge, where Alec was busy hammering an elegant gate for one of the fancy houses in Iron Creek. Garrett waved at him and waited for him to finish his task.

"Good morning to you," Alec said, taking off his gloves and setting them down on his bench.

"That looks quite ornate," Garrett said, moving closer to admire the smith's handiwork.

"For the Jellicoes. Their gate came down in the last storm."

"They're good people."

Alec nodded and pointed toward a bench nearby. The two men sat down. "What can I do for you?"

"I don't know if you have time and I know you are busy, but I have to leave town for a few weeks. My sheep are up in the summer grazing land, just up from my cabin. They don't need much, but it helps to check on them from time to time— make sure there's no coyotes or bobcats around."

"I'd be happy to," Alec said with a grin. "You going somewhere nice?"

"Just to Minneapolis," Garrett said, trying hard not to give too much away. He knew there would be questions when he returned with Mrs. White, but he'd rather put off having to answer them until then. Perhaps he'd know more about why he was bringing her here by then. "Thank you, Alec. I appreciate it. A lot."

"Glad to help."

The pair sat in silence for a few moments. It wasn't uncomfortable. Neither man was inclined to speak just to fill the space. Garrett stood up. "I'd best get on my way. I'll be leaving town tomorrow. Will hopefully return within a couple of weeks, though it might be longer depending on the weather."

"Safe travels," Alec said, standing up and offering his giant paw to Garrett to shake. Garrett was not a small man, but the blacksmith towered over him, and the man's heavily calloused hands made Garrett's look petite.

Garrett hurried home, where he packed a bag and wrote a letter to Mrs. White, then made his way back to Iron Creek, where the stagecoach would arrive outside the saloon at approximately four o'clock. If he was lucky, there would be a place on it, not just for his letter, but for himself as well. He paced nervously, praying that everything would work out. There was so much risk involved. What if she had been lying to him, preying on him to gain his sympathy? What if she was, as she seemed, one of the finest women he'd known—other than his mother and much-missed wife?

It was too late to have regrets, he decided, as the stagecoach rattled to a halt in front of him just fifteen minutes later.

He had started this, so he had to finish it. Whatever might happen had been set in motion from the moment he'd chosen to place that advertisement. He was going to meet the only woman who had replied—and he was sure that he liked her, at least what he knew of her. He could only hope that he wouldn't make a mess of everything once he was with her in person.

There was no room inside the stagecoach, but the driver offered him a place up top with him. The weather was fine, and Garrett would much rather be in the fresh air than cooped up inside, anyway. He didn't much like enclosed spaces, and those where there were lots of people made him uncomfortable beyond measure. And he wasn't a loquacious man. He used his words sparingly, and many took that for rudeness rather than reticence.

The driver was a man much like himself, it turned out. Born to an Ojibwe mother and a Swedish father, Nelson Gustavson, too, had never really felt at home in either world. And, like Garrett, he talked little, which was fine with them both. The coach stopped every twenty miles or so to swap horses and for passengers to embark and disembark. When they reached Grand Marais, the mail sacks were loaded onto one of the faster mail coaches, and Garrett prayed that his letter to Mrs. White would reach her in time and that she wouldn't have impulsively headed out without having heard from him.

By the time they reached Moose Lake, Garrett was sick of traveling. He'd never been fond of coaches. Riding alone on horseback was definitely preferable to this infinite cycle of stops and starts, unhitching and re-hitching the horses, chivvying the passengers out of the saloons before they'd finished their meals or still yawning from their beds as the driver didn't wish to stay anywhere longer than a few hours— and the endless horizon. Garrett didn't mind the last bit so much but being around people for so long was wearing on his nerves. He was getting grumpy and tired, as well as filthy and smelly. It would be necessary to ensure he was clean-shaven and better presented when he finally made it to Minneapolis as he did not want Mrs. White to think him a slovenly oaf.

Five days after its departure from Iron Creek, the stage-coach drew to a halt outside the station in Minneapolis just after nine o'clock in the morning. Garrett was glad to disem-bark. It had not been the most pleasant few days of his life. He wondered if there might be a more comfortable way to travel on the return journey as he did not want Mrs. White to hate Minnesota before she'd even had a chance to see it, and five days in a stagecoach might be enough to make her wish she'd never come.

As he stretched his limbs and reached for his bag, he wondered what would be best. In his heart, he wished to rush straight to the hotel he'd told Mrs. White to go to so he might meet with her immediately. He was so eager to have a face and a voice to go with the wonderful letters that they had shared, but a quick glance at his travel-stained clothes and bearded chin in a nearby shop window told him it would be wise to find a public bathhouse and a barber before he even thought about going anywhere else.

Garrett hated Minneapolis. It was too big and too loud,

with carts and carriages racing up and down the streets at all hours. People hurried everywhere, too busy to stop and say hello, and they looked askance at any face they did not know. He rarely felt at home anywhere, but he felt totally out of place and as unwanted as a deadly plague in places like this. And it was quiet and sedate in comparison with Chicago, which he had vowed long ago to never return to. He made his way through the crowds to the bathhouse and paid a few pennies for a hot bath.

Half an hour later, he emerged smelling of soap and dressed in his Sunday finest. He went to the barbershop next door and enjoyed the quiet sensation of the cut-throat razor against his skin, the soft soapy lather, and the dexterous snipping by the barber as he cut Garrett's hair. Looking and feeling like a different man, Garrett finally made his way to the Resting Place to see if Mrs. White had arrived.

## CHAPTER 9

*E*arly September 1878, Minneapolis, Minnesota

Garrett smiled as his old friend Arvind Grayson opened the door to his tiny hotel and ushered him inside. "I am glad to see you, Garrett," the now-retired old trapper said, shaking his head. "Your Mrs. White. She arrived here a few days ago. She was right as rain, but I don't know what happened. When my Alice went up to check on her, when she didn't come down for either supper or breakfast, the poor thing was in bed, white as the sheets, with a fever I've not seen the likes of in all my days."

"She's sick?" Garrett said, stunned. She had somehow managed to travel the entire length of the country, fleeing yellow fever, yet she had now succumbed to something?

Arvind nodded. "Alice is with her, and we've sent for the doctor, but she's weak as a kitten."

"May I see her?" Garrett asked, not sure if such a thing would be improper or not.

"I'll take you up," Arvind said. "Thankfully, we have no other guests, but I worry for my Alice."

"I understand," Garrett said. Alice was now in her seventies, same as Arvind. Both had always been as healthy as anyone you could ever wish to meet, but such things didn't always mean anything. Look at Mrs. White. She'd survived the outbreak of one of the deadliest diseases man had ever known, yet now she was sick.

Arvind showed Garrett upstairs, but he didn't come into Mrs. White's room with him. "Someone has to wait for the doctor," he said as he started back down the stairs. "And Alice insisted that at least one of us needed to stay well, should the worst happen."

"She's that bad?" Garrett asked anxiously, but Arvind had already disappeared back down the stairs.

Garrett knocked softly and entered the sick room. Alice stood to greet him, but she didn't embrace him as she would have done previously. "You stay back," she warned him. "It's best this doesn't spread, whatever it is."

He hovered in the doorway, staring at the slender figure of Mrs. White. He didn't know what he'd been expecting her to look like, but the tumble of golden curls that fell in lank strands on the pillow, the pale, pinched-looking cheeks, and the listless body were not it. Her eyes were closed, and she didn't seem to be aware of anything, though her chest rose and fell ever so slightly with each labored breath.

"She's been unconscious since last night," Alice explained.

"It happens when a fever runs this high. It came on so suddenly. She's been bright as a button since she got here, and so excited to meet you."

"She came from New Orleans," Garrett said. "You don't think it could be yellow fever? Could she have brought it with her?"

"No. She was perfectly well when she arrived. It's not likely influenza, but possibly pneumonia—the doctor will be here soon. Mrs. White seemed a strong kind of woman before she fell sick, so she'll pull through. Try not to worry."

"She's been traveling for months," Garrett said, though he did not know for a minute why he'd done so. Alice and Arvind already knew that. "She must be exhausted." They stood in silence for some time, Alice giving him a sad look, Garrett unable to take his eyes from the prone figure in the bed. After all this time, all their letters, this was their meeting. It did not feel fair or right. Mrs. White had gone through so much already just to get here.

The creak of the stairs announced the arrival of the doctor. He came into the room, his long black coat flaring behind him, and his hawklike nose and sharp eyes marking him as someone brilliant but not entirely caring. He briskly examined his patient, then turned to Garrett. "Influenza," he announced. "She'll need care, but she's young and the fever should break soon enough."

With that, he was gone. Garrett hadn't ever been much impressed by the competence of any doctors he'd come across, but this one seemed particularly cold and unfeeling, and no doubt would charge them a heavy fee for his visit, diagnosis, and lack of direction for Mrs. White's care. Garrett took a few deep breaths in an attempt to calm his temper. When he felt he had succeeded sufficiently, he turned to Alice. "I shall take her to my mother," he said.

"She's not well enough to travel so far," Alice protested. "Devil Track Lake is days away, even on the stagecoach. Anything you'd be able to take Mrs. White in would have to go much slower than that. No, she should stay here. I can care for her. She's no bother."

"No, I'll not have you wearing yourself out on our account. Arvind needs you, Alice," Garrett said firmly. "I'll buy a wagon and fill it with cushions. We'll make her as comfortable as we can, and I will take her to the Ojibwe. Zaagaasikwe will know how to heal her. They'll be at the summer hunting grounds, so not so far away."

"She could be dead before you get there," Alice said, the tone of her voice rising with her concern.

"I'll send a message on ahead," Garrett said. "There will be a hunting party near North Branch at this time of year. That's only a few days in a wagon from here. I think Zaaga said she'd be going as far as Island Lake. There'll be someone with healing skills on the way, someone that'll care a darn sight more than that old buzzard." Alice nodded reluctantly. Garrett could tell she wasn't happy about it.

But he would not leave Mrs. White's care to an elderly woman who would be at risk of her life should she get sick. The only people he trusted to care for Mrs. White properly were his family. He would get her to them, whatever it took. Zaaga was the most skilled healer he knew—and the only one he trusted with anything as important as Mrs. White's wellbeing.

He hurried out of the hotel and made his way to the marketplace. When he reached the covered area where ranchers and farmers brought their animals to be sold, he was delighted to find that a horse auction was taking place, and he snapped up a matching pair of bay cart horses for half the price he'd have expected to pay for them. "D'you know where I might buy a wagon for this pair to pull?" he asked as he made his payment to the seller.

"I'll give you one for free," the man joked, his ruddy face growing more so as he chuckled loudly. "Got one out the back there," he nodded toward the back of the barn. "Nobody wants it—it'll just be firewood otherwise." He glared at the horses as if they'd mortally offended him somehow. "But they're not good for that. Bad temperaments, both of 'em."

Cautiously, Garrett followed the horse trader toward the back of the barn. The horse trader's words echoed in his head. What was wrong with the animals? Garrett had looked them over carefully, and they were both sound, strong beasts, though a little fat. Both had seemed docile and sweet enough to him, and he was rarely wrong about such things. Yet this man had said they weren't suited. It didn't make sense.

And now he was offering a free cart, too? No man ever gave away anything worth having for free—at least, no man Garrett had ever known. Yet the wagon looked to be in reasonable condition. It was tired, needed a lick of paint and a few replacement planks perhaps, but the axles were good, as were the wheels. "There's no tarp for it," the man said as Garrett looked at the hoops that would once have held a thick canvas to cover the wagon. "But there's a man sells 'em just along the street."

Garrett crawled under the wagon, giving the undercarriage a very careful check, then got up and circled it once more. "I'll take it," he said. "If you'll throw in the horses' tack and harnesses."

The man grinned and stuck out his hand. The two men shook hands firmly to seal the deal. "You've done me a favor," the man said, moving to the far wall where a range of tack and harnesses hung from nails just overhead. He took down two bridles and driving bits, then reached for the wagon harnesses. "I'll be glad to see that pair of nags on their way, and this thing's been taking up space here for far too long."

Garrett didn't say anything. He just accepted the tack and took it over to the stall where his horses were waiting and watching, then he gentled them with soft words and clicks, patting their necks and rubbing their noses as he slipped on their bridles and harnesses. Neither horse made a fuss; they stood and let him do whatever he wanted, even as he led them toward the shafts of the old wagon and began to hitch them to it.

"My, my," the man who'd sold the horses said. "I've not ever seen them stand still or take the shafts that way in the year I've had them. I may have sold them too cheap." He stepped forward, and the horses reared and fidgeted, nickering and whinnying anxiously, their brown eyes wide, showing the whites in the corners. They were fearfully afraid of the man.

The man just chuckled. "Maybe not then." He walked

away, clearly delighted to have put one over on Garrett. Garrett shook his head; he would never understand that kind of man, the kind who only felt he'd done well if someone else did badly in a deal. It wasn't the way Garrett had been raised, and it certainly wasn't a way of doing business he would ever condone.

Despite the display of fear and agitation from his new charges, it took Garrett only a few minutes, once the man was gone, to gentle the horses once more. It was clear that they'd been badly cared for, and probably beaten by the horse trader, and that was why they were so afraid of him. After a bit of gentling, they were as docile and biddable as good cart horses should be. Garrett felt confident once more, and he led them out onto the street in the direction of the store the horse trader had told him about. In no time, he'd purchased himself a new tarpaulin for the wagon and had it fixed in place. He jumped up aboard and settled himself on the bench, clicking to the horses as he gently flicked the reins to get them to walk. They were perfect. They worked together well and didn't tug or pull. Garrett was relieved that his eye for horseflesh had been right, again.

His final stop was at a furniture shop, where he purchased a thick feather mattress and every cushion they had. He arranged them in the back of the wagon so that Mrs. White would feel like she was floating on air, then returned to the hotel where he lifted her up and carried her down the stairs as if she weighed no more than a feather herself. He and Alice got her settled, and Alice handed him a basket of food, several flasks of fresh water, and a tiny bottle of laudanum. "In case she wakes and is in pain," the kindly older woman said, folding his fingers over it. "I know you don't think it's a good thing, but it may be what she needs."

Garrett smiled and bent to press a kiss to Alice's plump cheek. "You are a wonderfully kind person," he said. "I cannot thank you enough for taking care of her."

"She's special, this one, isn't she?" Alice asked perceptively. "She reminds me a little of Oma. Not to look at, of course with all that blonde hair—and I mean before she got sick. When she arrived, she was so full of life. Exhausted, of course, after all that traveling, but she had that same zest for life, for experience."

"You think Oma had all that?" Garrett said, surprised that Alice would say such a thing. Oma had been sweet, kind, and tolerant; she'd put up with his nonsense and followed him from place to place as he tried to find where he belonged and never complained. He'd never much considered whether she'd thought their travels had been an adventure. Garrett had assumed that they were just something she had to endure to be with him.

"She did, and in spades," Alice said fondly. "A very brave woman, your Oma. She would have followed you anywhere, anyhow, she loved you so much, but she loved the places you went to, too. She enjoyed meeting all those new people, doing new things."

"I doubt that," Garrett said, frowning. "Most people we met on our travels were at best unkind, the rest were downright abusive to her. An Ojibwe in their midst was not to be borne."

"She didn't dwell on those ones. She made friends as easily as she smiled, with those open enough to see her," Alice said. "She had a way of looking at the world that meant she could always find the good in anyone and the positives in any situation."

Garrett couldn't argue with that. It was true enough. Oma had somehow managed to find happiness wherever she was. It was a gift that still eluded him. "She was a very special woman."

"And I think this Mrs. White is, too," Alice said. "Write to me. I want to know how she fares. Promise."

"I promise," Garrett said, clasping her hands in his and looking into her soft hazel eyes. "And I will take good care of her and get her to my mother quickly. She will get well. She has to—there's no way she came all this way to falter now."

## CHAPTER 10

*E*arly September 1878, Ojibwe Hunting Camp, North Branch, Minnesota

The sounds around her were unusual. Katy was sure she could hear drums, or maybe that was just her head pounding. The scent of smoke and peculiarly accented voices speaking words Katy had never heard before hung in the air. Her eyes slowly blinked open. The lids felt so heavy she could hardly lift them. Everything around her was blurred and swam in and out of focus, making her feel nauseous. She closed them again. She tried to take a deep breath, but her chest felt too tight, and it hurt to even try.

A cool hand gently rested upon her brow. "The fever has broken," a gentle female voice said. "She'll be back with us again soon." The voice had a strange accent to it, one Katy could not place. But she liked it; it was very soothing.

"You're sure?" a more anxious-sounding male voice said,

with the same unusual accent. "She's been unconscious for almost a week now."

"She's coming back to us, Aandeg. When have I ever been wrong?"

Katy tried to open her eyes again. She looked up into dark brown eyes, a gentle smile, and a face full of concern. "Wh-wh-where am I?" she asked nervously, her words coming out in a dry rasp. Her mouth had never been so dry. She swallowed and tried to lick her lips, which were cracked and dry, too. Then she reached up to rub at her throat, but her limbs were as heavy as lead, so she let her arm drop back to the bed.

The man moved closer. "Mrs. White don't fret. You are completely safe. I am Aandeg. This is my daughter, Zaagaasikwe. She has been caring for you. Waabshkizi…" he paused, realizing she might not recognize that name. "Garrett Harding is her son. You've been sick with influenza. Your fever has raged for almost a week. He brought you to us because he wanted you to get the best care."

"But where am I?" Katy asked again, trying to sit upright. She did not know these people with their strange names, and though they seemed to know Mr. Harding, she still hadn't met him.

The woman drew closer. "You are at North Branch, at our hunting camp, Mrs. White."

"But I was in Minneapolis, at the Resting Place," Katy said, her eyes now wide open. She looked around her. She seemed to be in a wigwam or teepee; Katy had never been entirely sure what they were called. It was made by stacking long branches propped upright and gathering them at their meeting point above her head. The structure was then covered with sheets of birch bark, which were light and rolled up easily. A fire flickered gently in the center of the structure and there were furs everywhere for warmth. The low bed she laid on was very comfortable and warm. An elderly man stood to her left, and a younger woman, though still old enough to have gray hairs at her temples, stood to her right.

"I am Garrett's mother," the woman explained. "When he arrived to meet you, he found you very sick. You've had a raging fever. Garrett was unhappy with the doctor in Minneapolis. He didn't want to risk anything happening to you, so he brought you here to me."

"That isn't strictly true," Aandeg said with a grin. "We were at Island Lake. Garrett insisted we leave and come to you as you were too weak to travel further."

"Where is he? I thought he would be here," Katy said, letting Zaaga settle her back down in the bed.

"He had to return to his herd," Aandeg said. "We assured him we would take care of you. Once you are well enough to travel, we will start the long journey back to Devil Track Lake. He will come to you there."

Katy felt her heart sink. She had been so looking forward to meeting Mr. Harding, and now, when he was the only person in this entire state that she knew even the tiniest thing about, he was not here. She wanted to cry. Katy was so tired, and every bit of her body ached with a dull heaviness that she had never before known. Then she remembered the child in her belly. She impulsively reached for her stomach, then realized that she could not let Garrett's family know before he did.

It would be wrong, so very wrong, if he were to find out that way.

Though, what if that was the reason he'd gone away? Perhaps his wise mother had seen the changes in Katy's body and told her son, and he'd been angry with her for not telling him? She closed her eyes and tried to hold in the tears that threatened to fall at the thought that she had ruined everything before it had even begun. She so wanted things to be different. She had so longed to make a good impression, and all Mr. Hardy had seen of her was a sick woman who hadn't told him the truth.

Aandeg left the shelter. Zaaga fetched Katy a drink of water. It felt cool and refreshing, but she was too weak to manage the cup alone, so the older woman had to help her take small sips to soothe her dry mouth and burning throat. "You are with child," Zaaga stated. It was not a question. It was the simple observation of a woman who had probably seen more births than Katy could imagine.

"I am," she said, seeing little point in denying it.

"And yet, my son did not mention it to me." Her voice was calm, still, but her rich brown eyes were narrowed slightly as she took Katy's measure.

"Because I have not yet told him," Katy admitted. There was something about this woman that made her speak the truth.

Zaaga nodded sagely. "I thought as much. He is a good man, but I am not sure how he might have reacted to such news. In that, he is like the white men who birthed him, I fear. They care too much about whose child is whose. Here, we are all of the tribe. All one people. Everyone is our mother, everyone our father." She moved to the fire and started to rip up some leaves and place them into a pot. She poured hot water over them and left the mixture to steep as she fetched a round cup with no handle.

"You don't think Mr. Harding feels that way?" Katy asked, her heart sinking into her boots.

"I think he is torn. When he left us to find his own people and to learn of his past, he learned many things. Some were good, some were bad. I pray that our teachings were strong enough to keep him straight. As a mother, you fear for your children, and perhaps I worry about him too much. But he has always been a troubled boy."

"I wanted to tell him," Katy said fervently as she watched Zaaga pour the pale golden liquid from the pot into the cup. "I just wasn't sure how to. I so loved receiving his letters and have been so excited to finally meet with him. Every time I'd go to write the words, I didn't know how to say them. Then I'd convince myself that it was the wrong time, and I would lose my nerve."

"There is never a right time for difficult news," Zaaga said wisely, bringing Katy the cup. "But I am glad to hear that you are as eager to meet him as he has been to meet you. Now, I want you to drink this. It is willow bark and raspberry leaf tea. It will ease the aches and pains and help you sleep." Katy did as she was told and drank the tea. She sank back against the soft furs and closed her eyes. She had never felt so bone-weary in all her life.

When she awoke, Zaaga was not in the shelter, and neither

was Aandeg. Feeling the need to go to the bathroom, Katy tried to pull herself up, but she was still too weak. She fell, causing a clattering of pans and pots as she stumbled. Zaaga came running. "You are not strong enough," she admonished Katy as she helped her up.

"I needed to…" Katy paused. It was not proper to say such things. But Zaaga seemed to understand and did not seem too concerned by it.

"Let me help you," she said kindly, putting a strong arm around Katy's waist and helping her to her feet. "I can either fetch you a pot or, if you think you can make it, there is a place not too far from here."

"I think it would be nice to see where I am," Katy said with a wan smile. "And perhaps getting up and moving will help my strength return."

Zaaga nodded her agreement, and taking much of Katy's weight, she assisted her out of the shelter into the fresh air. They walked slowly toward a place some way from the camp. Katy's legs felt wobbly and unreal, and she stumbled often, but Zaaga was patient and gentle. Katy had her first chance to look around at the land Mr. Harding had spoken of so highly. He was right to. The lake they were camping by was magnificent, a calm pool of blue that took Katy's already feeble breath away. The land was green and beautiful. It was very different from the fetid swamps and bayous of New Orleans.

She sighed. "It is as lovely as he said."

"It is our home, for better or worse," Zaaga said, looking around her as if seeing the place through new eyes. "It is ever changing, and it is up to us to take care of it for our children and their children yet to come."

Zaaga helped Katy to a sheltered spot and turned her back while she did what she needed to do. The relief Katy felt was incredible, and she doubted that she would ever do such a thing with such an outstanding view ever again. Something so mundane, so simple, was made magnificent by the incredible landscape.

After a slow but slightly improved walk back to the tent, Zaaga settled Katy back into bed and gave her more raspberry leaf tea. "Please don't tell Mr. Harding about the baby," Katy said urgently as she watched the woman preparing a rich venison stew for their supper. "I will tell him, I promise—but not yet. There is so much I am unsure of, and I do not wish to make anything harder than it already is."

"You do not have long before he will notice anyway," the older woman said. "Ojibwe grow up seeing one another in all ways, all the many changes that happen in our bodies. We don't hide things the way the white men do. His fear for you when he brought you here may have blinded him a little, but he will see the signs almost as easily as I have. You will need to do it soon."

Katy nodded. She knew that Zaaga was right, but she feared she might never find the words to tell Mr. Harding the truth, however much she wanted to. There was so much at stake, and so much that could now be taken from her. She had seen the beauty of this place, and she had finally felt the pull of place that Mr. Harding had spoken of in his letters. She belonged here. It was where she was supposed to be.

But as the days passed and he did not return, Katy grew worried. She needed to see Mr. Harding, to explain all the things she had left unsaid in her letters. Her body was healing and her limbs getting stronger with each passing day. With Zaaga's care and the good food prepared around the campfire each night, her baby was also thriving and growing at pace. If she did not tell him soon, he would work it out for himself, and that might make everything so much harder.

She took walks by the lake and had even ventured into it for short dips occasionally as the Ojibwe did. The water was bracingly cold, so she rarely stayed in long, but doing so made her feel fully alive in a way she'd not ever known before. Lying back, floating, and staring up at the sky was such a peaceful and soothing thing to do. She felt relaxed and at ease, and it did not take her long to settle into the rhythm of the Ojibwe.

She was so welcomed by everyone it surprised her. When she had woken up to see strangers—natives—she had been so frightened, even though she had known about Mr. Harding's upbringing. It was hard to banish a lifetime of news stories telling of the savagery of the tribes and how they would scalp a man as soon as help him. The Ojibwe were not a warlike people. They lived in harmony with the land and with each other.

Finally, Zaaga decided that Katy was strong enough to make the journey northwards, and so it was time to break camp. Katy watched the small group of hunters as they packed up their things with barely a word to one another. It was so practiced, so well-rehearsed—a task that had been undertaken a hundred times or more, so nobody needed direction except Katy. Within just an hour or so, the entire camp was packed up and loaded onto the horses and wagons, and the site itself looked as if nobody had ever been there.

As the small caravan of wagons and horses, men and women made its way north toward Island Lake, Katy was delighted to find herself able to do more and more each night when they settled in and each morning when they broke camp. She found her way into the tasks, so she soon needed no direction either. It felt good to be a part of it all, even though her task was so simple—to fill water vessels and pack them into the wagons. She took pride in it, and it helped her to feel a part of the tiny community she found herself in.

The Island Lake campsite was only a few days from Grand Marais, and she knew that Mr. Harding often went there to buy livestock and important items. He'd told her so in his letters. She hoped that it meant he might soon be with them. And she was right to be optimistic. They had been there barely an hour when Mr. Harding finally returned to fetch her.

Katy heard he had arrived long before she saw him. Everyone was excited to see him, and his friends and family crowded around him, offering affectionate hugs and teasing ribs. It was clear from the joking comments that his presence was a rare occurrence, and one that brought much pleasure. She held back, taking in every inch of his tall, muscular frame and handsome face. If he'd been dressed as the other Ojibwe, she could easily have mistaken him for one of them, with his thick, dark hair and tan skin. But he wore the clothes of the white man—jeans and a brushed cotton shirt, a Stetson, and a pistol holstered at his hip. He wore his hair shorter, too, and it had a curl that theirs did not. He had the dark shadow of stubble on his chin that few of the Ojibwe seemed to have. But his aquiline features were similar to those of his adoptive grandfather, Aandeg, and the warmth in his eyes was certainly that of his adoptive mother.

As he approached her, Katy had never been so nervous— not even when she'd told her parents of her intention to wed Jacob and follow him to New Orleans. Her belly was so swollen now that she didn't think it possible to ignore, even though her gown did its best to disguise it. However, Mr. Harding didn't look anywhere other than in her eyes. He smiled at her, his eyes lighting up with pleasure at the sight of her, and Katy felt her heart melt.

She had not expected it, but there was an immediate and deep connection between them. She couldn't have looked away from his face if she'd wanted to. The force of attraction she felt for him took her breath as his rich brown eyes stared deep into her soul. "I cannot tell you how happy I am to see you well again," he said, his rich baritone voice oozing over her like thick caramel. "We were very afraid that after everything you had survived, we might lose you. I knew my mother would take good care of you and bring you back to us."

# CHAPTER 11

*L*ate September 1878, Island Lake, Minnesota

Garrett could hardly tear his eyes from Mrs. White's unusual green eyes. She was so much more lovely than he could ever have imagined, as different from Oma as night from day but just as perfect in her own way. Her golden hair lay over her shoulders, and he longed to reach out and touch it, to see if it was as soft as those shiny undulating waves looked. But he held back. It would not do to frighten her. Her gaze was steady, and he felt a peculiar pull between them, something that gave him hope that there could be more there.

"It is good to finally meet you," she said, her brow furrowing slightly. "I am sorry I don't remember our first meeting."

He chuckled. "I'm not entirely surprised. You were very

unwell. We could always pretend that this is our first meeting, and in many ways, for you at least, it is."

"Thank you for bringing me here, to your family. They have been very kind and have taken good care of me," she said cautiously. "I was a little scared when I first woke up, but your mother and grandfather soon put me at ease."

"They do that," Garrett said proudly. He loved his adoptive family dearly. They opened their hearts to those in need often, not just to him. "I wanted to know you were safe and well cared for before I went back to make arrangements for someone else to take care of the sheep."

"Who had been caring for them while you came to fetch me?" she asked curiously.

"Alec Jenks," Garrett told her. "He's the town blacksmith, and a fine one. It was not fair of me to expect him to care for them indefinitely though, as he'd agreed only to do me a favor and check on them from time to time for a couple of weeks. I've hired a man to watch them now, so there is no hurry for me to return. I can stay here with you as you get stronger, help the tribe when they move to Devil Track Lake in a few weeks, and then I will take you on to Iron Creek."

Mrs. White nodded. She looked pleased with his plans. But then a cloud passed over her features and she looked suddenly concerned, her beautiful eyes wide. "What of the Jellicoes? Surely, they were expecting me to start work soon? I would not blame them if they decided to hire someone else."

"Mrs. Jellicoe's sister has been staying with them since the twins were born and will remain with them until you arrive.

They are happy to await your arrival. I assured them it will not be longer than a month."

"Oh, I am so glad. I have been so worried that they may not want me after all the trouble."

"You have hardly been trouble. I am just glad that you have recovered so well," Garrett assured her.

"I am still a little unsteady from time to time, but I am much improved. And it is all thanks to Zaaga. Could you suggest something I might do for her, that would not offend her, to show her my thanks?"

Garrett was touched that she was so grateful and wanted to do something to show that to his mother. He had been sure she was a good person, but this confirmed it for him. "We could perhaps go fishing and catch some siscowet for her supper. It is her favorite. I can assure you that would please her greatly." Garrett smiled, amused that Mrs. White had so quickly understood his mother was not the kind to need praise or gifts for her kindness. She did as she did because it was who she was, but it didn't stop her from being touched by subtle shows of affection.

"Siscowet? I've not ever heard of that before," Mrs. White said, her brow wrinkling again. It was rather endearing that her face so easily showed her feelings, whether that be happiness, confusion, or puzzlement.

"It is what you might call lake trout. It is very delicious, and though it isn't the best time of year for it, we might be lucky if we take some rods and give it a try."

"I have never fished before," she said looking excited now. Her eyes were bright and her smile broad. "I have learned so many new skills since I have been here. Will you mind teaching me another?"

"Not at all," Garrett said, meaning every word. It would be a pleasure to spend some time with Mrs. White and get to know her better. "Aandeg keeps some rods by the shelter. I shall fetch them and ask Zaaga for some food for a picnic, and perhaps we could make an afternoon of it?"

She beamed, revealing tiny dimples in her cheeks that he'd not noticed before. "That would be lovely."

He took off his hat and bowed his head politely before leaving her to fetch what they would need. Garrett couldn't stop himself from looking back at her. She stood peering out over the lake with a serene look on her face. It was such a difference from the pale, gray skin and sweat-drenched visage he'd first encountered. She had filled out, too. His mother had no doubt been doing her best to feed Mrs. White to strengthen her. And it had worked. While she could never be called plump, Mrs. White was curvaceous in all the right places.

Zaaga smiled when he asked her for some food to take with them and packed a large basket full of some of her tastiest treats. Garrett found Aandeg's rods and nets and checked them over before returning to his mother. "We won't be long, I know there are chores to be done," he said.

She smiled knowingly and put a gentle hand upon his. "You take all the time you need. I am sure the two of you have much to talk about. We will see you both at supper."

Garrett kissed the top of her head, then took the basket of food and the fishing equipment and went back to where he had left Mrs. White. She was sitting on the ground, not seeming to notice or care that her pale blue dress might stain. He liked that. Fussy women had never been his type. He wasn't untidy, nor unclean, he simply didn't see the need for everything to be immaculate at all times. Katy looked up at him as he approached, raising her hand to shade her eyes from the autumn sun. She squinted a little, making her nose wrinkle like a rabbit's. She was very sweet indeed.

"Here, let me help you up," he said, setting his things down and offering her his hand. She took it and smiled.

"Thank you, Mr. Harding," she said. She brushed her skirt down, then bent to pick up the fishing rods.

"There's no need," he assured her. "I can manage."

"I have to build my strength. If I do not at least take something, I shall be slowing my recovery," she said with a cheeky grin. She'd obviously learned Zaaga's lessons by heart. His mother had always been firm about continuing to improve, not ever taking a backward step.

"Then you may help," he said grinning back. "I would not wish to upset my mother. She is a fearsome sight to see when riled."

"I can imagine. She is a strong woman," Mrs. White said, admiringly. "I can only hope to be as wise and determined."

"I'd say you have the determined part already," Garrett said a little shyly. "It takes a lot of courage to go through all you have and come out the other end of it."

"I wouldn't say that. I think I've just set one foot in front of the other and hoped the path might lead me somewhere," she said with a laugh. The sound of it was like a peal of bells, pretty and light and full of joy. Garrett couldn't keep from smiling. He could listen to her laugh all afternoon and not tire of it.

He led her along a narrow, lightly worn path that took them around the lake shore, away from the camp. By the water's edge, on a sheltered beach, was a canoe. He stowed everything they'd brought with them inside it and took the craft to the water's edge. Mrs. White didn't complain or look surprised by the nature of the boat, or the flimsiness of its construction. She just hitched up her skirts, waded into the shallows, and took her place in the craft.

"I don't think I've ever seen a white woman get in a canoe without so much as a squeal before," he said admiringly as he got in and pushed them off onto the water. He took up the paddle and began to propel them forward, but it was hard to steer with just one paddle. Mrs. White had obviously seen that they were veering to one side and then another as he paddled.

"I may have never been in one of these, but I used to enjoy the rowing boats on the lake in the park as a girl," she said, picking up the other paddle and starting to dip it into the water. "I am sure I can pick this up and be of some help at least."

"I'm sure you can, too," he said, his admiration growing with every minute in her company. "We'll paddle out to where the trees overhang the lake, over there." He pointed to a clump of trees nearby. "There's usually good fishing around their roots."

She nodded, and they paddled to where he'd indicated. He showed her how to cast her line. On the first attempt, her line caught on the roots of one of the trees and almost capsized them. Garrett laughed and said, "Don't worry, that's part of fishing". He explained again what she should do, and she tried a second time. This time, her bait fell from the tiny, barbed hook at the end of her line before it had even reached the water. But on the third attempt, Garrett beamed at her. She'd obviously done it right.

After that, the pair sat in silence, enjoying the unusually warm autumn sunshine and the peace and quiet out on the lake. It seemed that any hope of catching a fish was gone as the afternoon drew to a close, but they had enjoyed a delicious picnic and Mrs. White seemed delighted to have learned a new skill, even if she'd been unsuccessful at it. They were just about to pack up and go when something bit at Garrett's line. He struck his rod and reeled in a perfect, large lake trout. Mrs. White clapped her hands happily. "Oh, it is so lovely," she said, admiring the way the scales reflected the sunlight, making it seem as though the fish was made entirely of tiny mother-of-pearl flakes.

"It will taste lovely, too," Garrett said grinning. "Shall we head back?"

She nodded. "Can we cook it for your mother? Do you think she will let us near her fire? She so often refuses to let me help her cook, but she has so many ways of doing things that I would love to learn."

"I'm sure I can convince her," Garrett assured her. "And I will let her know you wish to learn. She is a good teacher and will be honored by your interest."

They made their way back to shore. As Garrett helped her out of the boat, he felt his skin prickle with desire when his warm hand took hers. He had not expected to be attracted to anyone again. He had been sure that he would never love anyone in the way he had Oma, but there was no denying that something was sparking between them. Mrs. White was such easy company and such a joy to behold, with her blonde curls and bright green eyes.

She watched him, fascinated, as he gutted and cleaned the fish before they made their way back to the camp. Katy was obviously tired, but she fought against the yawns. She did not want to miss one moment, like a small child fighting against itself to experience every moment. It was rather sweet. By the time they were back at the campfire, she could no longer stop her eyes from closing. "You should rest," Garrett said softly. He took her arm gently and guided her toward Zaaga's shelter. "We can cook this and give it to my mother at supper when you wake."

"But—" Mrs. White started to protest.

"Rest is as important as building your strength. I am sure my mother has told you that," he said firmly. She smiled, and he knew that Zaaga had indeed stressed the importance of sleep to her when she had been determined to push herself too hard.

"Just an hour," she said. "You must wake me in time to help you prepare the fish for your mother."

"I shall," he promised fervently. "I will need your help, or the fish will be burned to a cinder."

# CHAPTER 12

*E*arly October 1878, Leech Lake, Minnesota

Zaaga was delighted with her fish when Garrett and Katy presented it to her. She spoke of how delicious it had been for many days afterward and always smiled warmly at Katy as she did. Yet there was still the unspoken warning in her eyes that Katy should tell Garrett about the baby. Katy knew that she was a mother looking out for her beloved son and that she should have told him long ago, but it grew harder and harder to do with every passing day.

She had come so close to telling him the day they went fishing. She had seen such sincerity in him, and she had no more doubts that he would make a fine husband and an excellent father. That she had not told him made her feel terrible, and she was sure that Zaaga had expected her to. She hated that she had been a coward and not been as honest and open with him as he had been with her.

The Ojibwe had started to talk about moving on from Island Lake, and people were starting to get ready for the next stage of their journey back to their homelands around Devil Track Lake. Katy and Mr. Harding spent time together every day. He called on her in the morning, usually with a small posy of whatever wildflowers he could find. At lunch, he chose to always sit by her side and he came to meet her each evening at Zaaga's shelter to take her to supper with the entire tribe around the campfire.

Katy couldn't help liking him. He was sweet and kind, very generous, and from what she'd seen as he played with the children of the tribe, he was patient and gentle with them. He taught them skills as well as roughhousing with them. He played catch and hide-and-go-seek, always pretending not to see the easily visible arm or leg that gave away most of the children's hiding places. He was respectful of his elders and was happy to help anyone. He was obviously well-loved, though from the way he spoke sometimes, Katy feared that he did not know that.

As the time drew near for them to pack up and leave once more, Katy had butterflies in her belly. This move would mean she too would be going to her new home—to Iron Creek. She would meet her new employers and have to admit to them that she was with child and might not be able to help them out for as long as they might have hoped. When Mr. Harding had returned and she'd asked after them, she had secretly hoped that they might have decided to take on other help. It would have been easier for her that way.

And she still needed to tell Mr. Harding. Zaaga had not

mentioned it again, but Katy knew that the older woman was waiting, almost as nervously as she was herself, to see her son's reaction to the news. It wasn't something that was easy to bring up in conversation, though. Katy had so hoped that there would be a moment, clearly defined and easy to spot, that would tell her when it was time to let him know.

But she also hoped that he might say something first. To her, her burgeoning belly was an obvious sign not to be missed, yet nobody but Zaaga had seemed to notice it. In the early days, that had been more understandable, but not now, unless Mr. Harding simply thought her plump, which was quite possible. She certainly seemed to be eating far more than she could ever remember, which might make anyone who did not know her think that such an appetite was normal for her.

"We leave tomorrow, Mrs. White," Garrett said, as they walked to supper that evening. "In just four, perhaps five days, we shall be in Iron Creek."

"That's wonderful," Katy said, but even she could hear the anxiety in her voice.

He offered her his arm. "You're nervous?" he asked as she tucked her arm through his.

"A little," she admitted. "I have traveled before and started anew in a city where I knew nobody, but I had my husband by my side. I suppose it did not feel so daunting as I knew that I had Jacob, whatever else happened."

Garrett paused. "I had not thought on it much. I should have; I am sorry. The Jellicoes are fine people. You will like them a lot, I am sure. And you must remember that you do know me, and I can assure you I will never be more than a short ride away if you need me." He patted her hand where it lay upon his arm.

"Thank you," she said softly, but it didn't take away her fear. She knew that she still had to tell him about the baby. Would he be just a short ride away from her then?

They ate their meal, a rich hearty stew, and Mr. Harding escorted Katy back to Zaaga's shelter. She knew that she had been unusually quiet all night and was sure that he was probably wondering if there was more to her confession about her nervousness than she'd let on. She'd said that she'd not been so afraid when she moved to New Orleans because she had been married and had her husband by her side. Perhaps, he thought, she was hinting to him that she would like that to be the case again?

In all his dealings with her, it seemed to Katy he was determined not to be too forward with her, though she was sure that he had been as strongly attracted to her from the first as she had been to him. She knew well enough that she was pretty, comely, and very sweet. Jacob had told her so often, as had many others throughout her life. Her looks meant little to her, though. Katy would much rather Mr. Harding found her fascinating company. She hoped that her tales of her travels and her life in New Orleans amused him, and she tried to make them light-hearted and fun.

But though she was sure she liked him and was almost certain that he liked her in return, she couldn't help asking herself if she was truly ready to be wed once more? Mr. Harding seemed determined to let her dictate the speed and intensity of their peculiar courtship. He had told her that he did not want her to feel she had to make any kind of commitment to him, and he knew all too well that she had only just lost her husband, mere months earlier. It would not be right to push her too quickly into anything new.

She watched him every moment, always wondering what he might be thinking, especially now. He had already turned away from her, leaving her at the doorway as he always did, and she was halfway inside the shelter when he spun on his heel and hurried back. "Would you marry me," he blurted, then fell silent, hanging his head and biting at his lip as he waited nervously for her answer.

She turned back to face him. "Wh-what did you just say?" she asked, looking stunned.

Mr. Harding took a long, deep breath. "I asked if you would marry me. I know it is too soon after your husband's passing, and that we barely know each other, but I fell in love with you from your letters and knowing you in person has only made me love you more. I want you to be my wife. Perhaps if you were, it might ease your fears about your new life in Iron Creek."

"My goodness," she said, nodding her head slowly and trying to calm her suddenly racing heart. "I did not mean you to feel you have to do this when I said what I did earlier."

"I know you did not. And I can assure you that I am not asking you because of that. At least, not in regard to my feelings. I do not know how you feel about me, but I hope that I am not too hideous a prospect when it comes to marriage. I can assure you that I would never insist upon anything, even if we are wed, that you do not wish for. I long only to be with you and enjoy your company as I have done in these past days. It has been wonderful knowing that the first and last person I will see each day is you. I look forward to hearing about everything you've done and all the things you've learned. You have become so very dear to me, and I want you to be my wife so we can do this every single day of our lives."

Katy was tongue-tied, though it seemed that the usually taciturn Mr. Harding was not. She'd never heard him say so much all at once, and all of it was so lovely and romantic. He was saying everything right, and his affection for her was so pure. It made her feel rotten inside. She was lying to him, and she should have told him from the start. Katy should at least tell him now. But instead, she simply said, "Yes, I'll marry you. I would be delighted to marry you."

Mr. Harding dipped his head and pressed a tentative kiss to her lips. "Good night, Katy. I may call you Katy now, I hope?"

She nodded and smiled. Her name sounded lovely upon his lips. "Good night, Garrett," she said. As if he was worried that she might change her mind, he hurried away, back to his own shelter. Katy stared after him and berated herself for her cowardice. If there had ever been a moment when she should have told him the truth, it was the moment that had just passed between them. She was a terrible person. She did not deserve to be so loved, or so obviously respected. Garrett Harding was too good for her.

When she went inside, Zaaga was sitting by the fire. From the look on her face, she had heard everything. "I want to say I am happy for you, but he still does not know, does he? He is so blind that he doesn't see anything more than you."

"I did not mean for it to be this way," Katy said. The last thing she wanted was for this wonderful woman to despise her for her weakness. "I love him, too. I did not know if that was possible after losing Jacob. I certainly did not expect to have such strong feelings for anyone so soon. But the longer I have left it to tell him, the harder it gets. And as you say, he only sees what he wants to see."

"There is no more putting it off. You must tell him before you are wed. It would not be fair to him if you do not."

"I know," Katy agreed. "But how do I say it without losing his love and respect forever?"

"That is for you to work out. I cannot tell you how to tell my son such a thing. Only you must do so, for both your sakes."

Katy turned and ran out of the shelter into the night. She ran toward Garrett's, but when she got there, she didn't dare announce herself. Instead, she turned and ran toward the lake. Katy sat down on the pebbled beach and watched the water gently lapping at the stones. It was peaceful and quiet, unlike her thoughts. She fidgeted with the silver band on her ring finger. "Oh, Jacob, what mess have I gotten myself into this time?" she asked the sky above her. "If only you were here to tell me what I should do. You were always the sensible one, even though my parents thought otherwise. You never did an impulsive thing in your life. You thought everything through so carefully, planned everything that could go wrong, as well as those that might go right. You were my rock, my anchor."

She picked up a couple of smooth pebbles from the shore and stood up to throw them out across the water. She flicked her wrist the way her father had taught her as a girl to make them bounce along the surface before finally dropping out of sight. She found the repetitive action and the sounds of the skipping stones calming, but she wasn't yet ready to go back to her bed. She could not face Zaaga. Instead, she made her way back to the camp, grabbed some furs from the stores, and settled down by the campfire. She stared into the flames, letting them clear her thoughts as the crackle and snap of the fires soothed her to sleep.

# CHAPTER 13

*E*arly October 1878, on the road to Devil Track Lake, Minnesota

Katy was quiet as the tribe moved on. Garrett was concerned for her and wondered if perhaps she had not recovered as fully as she had seemed to. He was also concerned that, despite the fact she would be introduced to her new home as his fiancée, she was still anxious about it all. Whenever he asked her about it, she dismissed his concerns, saying simply that she was tired. It didn't stop him worrying, though, and the more he fussed over her, the more she seemed to withdraw from him.

He simply couldn't understand it. She had seemed so delighted and accepted so readily when he had proposed. Yet now she was treating him as if he were a stranger. It didn't make sense. He spoke to his mother, but she simply said that Katy would tell him what was wrong in her own time, though it was clear that Zaaga knew something she wasn't telling him too. He had never liked secrets. That his mother and Mrs. White, the two people who just days ago he would have said he trusted more than anyone else in this world, were the ones keeping something from him made it even harder to bear.

When they finally drew close to Iron Creek, Garrett was relieved. He would be able to see Katy settled into her accommodations with the Jellicoes, then enjoy the peace and quiet of his own home, where perhaps he might be able to make some sense of everything. But he doubted he would. He had not changed. Whatever was wrong was something that concerned Katy, and he had to respect her and trust that she would tell him in time.

Katy wanted to tell him, but it got harder and harder with every day that passed. Zaaga stopped mentioning it, but she had a look on her face every time she saw Katy, a look that made Katy feel judged and found wanting. She hated that. She had grown so very fond of the older woman and respected her so much. To have lost Zaaga's respect hurt almost as much as losing her own parents had all those years ago.

And she missed them still. Every time she thought about Garrett's proposal, she longed to be able to speak with them, to tell them, to have them be there to see it. It seemed unfair that she would have a second marriage they would know nothing about and a child they might never meet. She would not have changed her time with Jacob for anything, but the loss of them pained her still.

She had chosen to ride in the back of one of the wagons. It gave her a little more privacy and meant that Garrett, on his horse, could not easily talk with her. It wasn't exactly comfortable, though he had done all he could to make it as soft and cushioned as he possibly could. Her trunk was by her head. She kneeled up and opened it, pulling out some paper, a pen, and some ink that Mrs. Havermeier had gifted her. Katy had placed the items carefully in a small wooden box Jacob had made for her for her birthday so they would remain safe on her remaining travels.

She sat back down and began to pour out her heart to her parents, writing down everything she longed to be able to tell them, everything she'd been too afraid or proud to admit to in the polite letters she had sent to them during her marriage to Jacob. She doubted if she would ever mail it, but it was cathartic to let all her thoughts out in a torrent. Katy told them about everything that had happened since she had walked out of their house all those years ago without polishing any of it to make it seem better or happier than it had been. She told them of her struggles and of the pain she had felt upon losing Jacob, and she told them of their grandchild and how she wished they might know him. Finally, she told them the date that she and Garrett had chosen to be their wedding day.

Katy put it in an envelope and addressed it as if she had every intention of sending it, then tucked it into her handbag. She could decide what to do with it later—she would probably burn it. But for the moment, it was an item of possibility. If sent, it might bring her parents back into her life or it might push them further apart, but for the time being, it had helped her to get her thoughts clear, and that was something she had needed to do for too long.

She had not dared to think too often of Jacob's passing or of their lives together before that in the months that had passed since that day. It hurt too much. They had been young, but their love had been strong and true. It had been hard enough just getting through every day without letting herself mourn him, but she knew she needed to. Yet she did not wish Garrett to think that her sudden melancholy was in any way his fault or that she cared for him any less because her thoughts were suddenly filled with her husband, her child's father. Perhaps her reluctance to tell Garrett of the baby had something to do with that. While she had not been able to deny that the child was growing and kicking inside her, she had needed to block out how that child had come to be.

No matter how wonderful a father any man choosing to come into her life might be, her child would never belong to them. He, or she, would always be Jacob's—a lasting reminder of the love she and her first husband had shared. But would Garrett be able to accept that? Would any man? She knew she was not being fair. She should have told him in her very first letter, and she should have told him on a hundred different occasions since. But she had not, and now he would think her a liar, out to manipulate him just to get her child a father.

But Katy loved him. It had crept up on her, but her feelings were as strong and true for Garrett as they had ever been for Jacob. It was too soon. It felt right and wrong at the same time. But it was the simple truth. She loved Garrett.

Katy could not bear to think that he might consider her capable of misleading him and manipulating him into marrying her, yet in so many ways, that was precisely what she had done. No matter how or when she told him now, it could only ruin everything. She didn't want it to be that way. She wished she could turn back the clock and change all of it. But she could not. And now, she must face the consequences. She just prayed that whatever it cost her, it did not hurt Garrett Harding too badly. He did not deserve that.

They stopped by a river later that evening. The next day, she and Garrett would part company with the Ojibwe. The Indians would continue on toward Red Lake while she and Garrett made their way to Iron Creek, Katy's new home. As they made camp, Garrett approached her looking a little nervous. She smiled at him, but his expression made the butterflies in her belly start to flutter uncomfortably. Perhaps Zaaga had grown tired of waiting for Katy to tell her son the truth and done it for her. Perhaps he was regretting his spontaneous proposal.

"I know this is perhaps a little sudden, but given my heritage, I would like to receive a blessing from the Ojibwe for our marriage," he said quietly. "It may be some time before we can arrange for a ceremony in the church in Iron Creek, and I am sure that you will not consider us wed until that can be arranged, but would you honor me by having a binding ceremony in Devil Track Creek? I would be happier when we must part ways if I know that we are promised to each other."

Katy laughed nervously. It was not what she'd been expecting. "I should like that," she said. "I want you to feel that we are wed in the way that means something to you as well as the one that matters to me."

He smiled, obviously relieved that she did not mind that he wanted to honor his upbringing in such a way. Katy knew that this was the moment she had been waiting for. It was time to be honest with him. Yet still, she could not bring herself to tell him. Instead, she let him tuck her arm through his and take her for a walk along the riverbank. He pointed out places he had played as a boy, the spot where he'd broken his wrist falling from a tree, and his mother's favorite place to gather a specific herb that she relied on to help those with fevers.

He seemed to enjoy watching her expression as he showed her the places he so loved. She had fallen as easily in love with the rugged landscape that surrounded them as she had with him. She hoped that he was glad that she was undaunted by his upbringing and the peculiar heritage he brought with him. She enjoyed his tales of boyhood, comparing the differences between his upbringing and her own. There was so much that was similar, yet so many things that set them apart.

He took off his jacket and laid it on the ground so she might sit when they reached a particularly beautiful part of the river where it bent and changed direction, creating a small pool at the turn. Overhanging trees offered shade and places for boys to climb and swing out into the river. "I should tell you of Oma," Garrett said cautiously. "I know you know something of my first wife, but perhaps it is time I tell you all."

Katy swallowed nervously. "There is no need," she said quickly.

"No, there is. I am not an easy man. You should know that before we are to be wed. I know that we will not be married in your eyes until a minister pronounces us wed, but for me, our commitment will be made tomorrow before my family and those with whom I have grown up. So, I think it best if we are honest with each other before we make any further promises to each other."

Katy wondered if he was doing this because he suspected something was wrong. She knew that she had been distant since his proposal and that he had noticed it. He had tried so hard to draw her out. Now, he was going for the more obvious approach by baring his own soul. "If you wish," she told him, her tone curt as she tried to hide her own fear that he was bringing her own confession closer.

"Oma was a wonderful woman," Garrett said with a wistful smile on his handsome features. "I loved her from when we were children, and she loved me. But she had a free spirit. She would never have settled anywhere, I don't think. She was happy to follow me, to travel as I did to earn money as a trapper and trader. But there were times when I had to leave her behind, and she had always cared for our friend Dibikad."

"She was untrue?" Katy said, annoyed on his behalf. He had surely not deserved that, no matter how long he might have been away. He was kind and good. And he spoke of this woman with such love. She must have been a fool to even think of choosing another man in his stead.

"I was rarely with her for almost a year," Garrett explained. "Even when I was present, I was a hundred miles away, trapped in my own thoughts and fears much of the time. I think anyone would have been lonely."

"That does not seem to be a good enough reason to me," Katy said.

"But you are a white woman, brought up to believe that fidelity is the most important of the marriage vows. To the Ojibwe, things aren't so straightforward, so black and white," he explained. "It was not her infidelity that hurt me. It was that she chose a man I had entrusted with her care in my absence. Dibikad was my dearest friend. He was like a brother in many ways, and it was his betrayal, far more than hers, that hurt. He broke his promise to me to protect her and keep her safe from those that might seek to take advantage of my absence. I had pride enough to be angry at that."

"Any man would," Katy said, surprised he could be so sanguine about his wife lying with another man. She did not know a single man who could be that way. At best, all the men she'd ever known would probably have shot the man and divorced the wife who did such a thing.

"The last year of our lives together were spent fighting constantly, and I did not even know about her feelings for Dibikad then. But I struggled with what I had put her through. I made her an outcast among her own people—the woman who chose a white man. We were not wanted in the towns either. She was bullied and reviled, and she had a terribly hard time. At least here she was loved. I sent her away from me for her own sake.

"Too late," Garrett said sadly, I learned of Ano "Oma died giving birth when the child came early. I was not there with her. I blamed myself. Knew that it was my fault. If I had been a better husband, she would have not been so angry, so concerned as she carried our son. He was so small, too small to survive, though he was named and accepted by the tribe. I thought that Dibikad was coming to console me after the burial. When he told me of their love, it tore me apart, especially when it meant that my son, my Ano, might have been his and not mine at all. I loved that boy, though he only lived a few days, and it still hurts that I may never know if he was truly mine."

"It must hurt you greatly." Katy reached out and placed a supportive hand upon his arm. "But it does nothing to change my feelings for you."

He placed his hand over hers and looked into her eyes. "It still hurts from time to time. There are days when I become melancholy and withdrawn. You should know that because I do not want you to ever think it is due to anything you may have done. I want to be a better husband to you than I was to Oma."

"I will remember that," Katy said, nodding. She blinked anxiously and gulped a few times before continuing. "But I have something I must share with you, too. I should have told you from the first and I hate that I did not. Please, forgive me. I never intended for things to be this way."

"You can tell me anything," he assured her. He had just told her that he felt responsible for his beloved Oma's passing, and because of it, the loss of his son. Garrett had told her that he still held bitter and proud thoughts, that he was a jealous man, yet he seemed calm, as though there was nothing she could tell him that would be harder to bear than that. Perhaps he was right, but Katy couldn't help thinking that the tale he'd just told her made her confession even harder.

She took a deep breath and closed her eyes as if she could not bear to look upon his expression. "I am with child," she said as she pulled her dress tight against her obviously swollen belly. Garrett stared at her swollen belly as if seeing it for the first time. His eyes widened and his jaw dropped open as if he could hardly believe that he could have missed seeing it. "It is my husband's. I think it is due to arrive in December."

# CHAPTER 14

*E*arly October 1878, Near Devil Track Lake, Minnesota

Garrett sat silently for a moment. He stared directly ahead, unable to look Katy in the eye. Memories of Oma looking so proud when she'd told him they would have a child flooded his mind. But he had not been ready, not really. He'd feared how a child of their mixed heritage might be received by both the Ojibwe and the townsfolk. It was not a decision to be taken lightly, and they had argued about it so many times. But it had seemed that the decision had been taken from them.

And then, after her passing, he had learned the truth. His jealous heart could not bear the thought that she had taken solace in another man's arms while he'd been away, and even worse, that she had not cared enough about him to tell him the simple fact that a child she expected him to raise might not be his. Oma had seen no fault in the child's possible parentage. She would have loved it, whether it was his or Dibikad's. Not knowing whose it might be, it seemed she felt that wasn't something important enough to share with Garrett.

At that moment, he had known that he should never have left her, no matter how hard it would have been to take her with him every time he had to journey further away. She had been too lovely, too warm to be alone for so long. He did not blame her or Dibikad. The fault had been his. He was not an easy man and never had been. But it had also shown him the darkest parts of himself, revealing things he would rather have never known.

And all of them had been so very young—though they'd believed themselves to be so wise, so ready for life and all it might hold. He had tried very hard to not mind. Yet now when he recalled his wife, he thought of the many times he had seen Oma smile Dibikad's way. He had forgotten all the perfect moments the two of them had shared. He forgot the friendship he and Dibikad had been so blessed to have. When he thought of either of them, Garrett couldn't help but see the image of a child with his wife's warm brown eyes and Dibikad's strong limbs. He could never picture a baby that resembled him and could not recall Ano's real features at all.

He stood up and looked down at Katy as if he intended to say something. But he could not find the words. He stormed away from her and did not look back. There was too much to say, yet nothing he could imagine saying. Was it his fate to never have his own child? Had he been cursed while still a baby? He had lost his parents when he was barely five years old, and he'd lost his wife and his child, though he would really never know if Ano had been his. And now, the woman he had so rashly let himself fall in love with was to have another man's child. And she had not told him. Was he destined to never have a family of his own, something to truly belong to him?

Of course, he knew that she had been married before she came to Minnesota. He knew she had felt strongly that she had to escape. Now it was all too clear why she had so needed to get away from New Orleans and the disease ravaging it. Any parent would do the same to protect their unborn child. And she had every right to be carrying another man's child, her husband's child. He could not blame her for that. But she had lied to him. Was he again to be the outsider in his own family, to never know the truth before it was too late?

He had always felt that way. No matter how much love Aandeg and Zaaga had given him, he knew that he wasn't theirs. He did not belong to them in the same way that his sister Diindiisi did. She had been born to Zaaga. She was of their blood. She belonged. He would never truly be Ojibwe. He was a white man raised by the tribe. His name marked his difference. His skin, the curl in his hair, the shape of his eyes had always told him he was different.

And now, he would be wed to a woman with a child he had not been expecting. She had lied to him from the start; she must have known. No, perhaps she had not lied. But she hadn't told him. And that was in some ways even harder to bear than his assumption that Oma must have believed that a man should not care whether a child was his or not. Even among the Ojibwe, he was certain that no man wished for his hearth mate to lie with someone else, to have a child with him. He was not sure if that had been Oma's thought, and he would never know, but he had no other explanation for her not telling him the truth. He had always been sure of that, and that was why he had been so angry with her.

As always, when faced with strong emotions he could not bear to feel, he could not face them immediately. He knew he had asked Mrs. White to be his bride, and he cursed to himself silently for having so impulsively sent word to his grandfather asking to have the ceremony that would join them in the eyes of the Ojibwe. Now he would have to tell his family, who had been so happy for him, that their hopes were to be dashed once more. As always, he was not destined for happiness, for the kind of life that other men seemed to have come to them so easily. He could not stay around yet another woman who had thought he was fool enough not to care. He couldn't even look at her.

Katy watched him leave. Tears began to pour down her cheeks. She had feared that he would be unhappy, that he might be angry with her even, but not that he would just leave her sitting there alone. His expression had changed so quickly, it was as if a dark cloud had passed across the sun. She sniffed loudly, wiped her eyes with her sleeve, stood up, and made her way back to the shelter she shared with Zaaga. The older woman was preparing food over the fire. She looked up and saw Katy's red eyes and the streaks on her cheeks.

"You told him," she said, standing and embracing Katy

warmly. "I hoped he might not take the news too badly, but I think it may have been a disaster."

"You might say that," Katy admitted, feeling the tears she'd only just managed to get under control begin to fall over her cheeks once more. "He told me a little more about his wife, and baby Ano. He told me he blames himself for their deaths."

"I feared that was the case," Zaaga said, nodding her head. "He has never truly come to terms with everything that happened then. I think it did not help that Oma chose a man of the Ojibwe. Perhaps if she had chosen a white man, it might not have hurt Garrett so much. But that she chose one of her own, though I cannot know for certain..." she trailed off. "Poor Waabshkizi never felt like he belonged with us. But he never felt like he belonged with your kind either."

"And I have made it worse," Katy said sadly, pulling away from the embrace of Garrett's mother. "I brought another man's child and expected him to accept that, though I never thought it would matter as it does."

"You love him?"

"I do. I did not expect that when I wrote to him. When Garrett said he would help me find a position, that there would be no expectation of a relationship, but that he would help me, I assumed that my not telling him about the child would not be a problem. If there was no relationship, my child was of no importance. But as we wrote to each other, we grew close... At least I believed we had."

"I think that is true. He would not have asked you to be his wife if he did not care for you. He is not one to do that. He is, in his own way, happy alone," Zaaga said. "He has not shown any desire to take a wife since he lost Oma. I was surprised when he told me he'd taken my advice to advertise for a bride."

"I should have told him in that first letter. I should never have convinced myself it would not matter," Katy said, putting the few things not in her bags back into them. "And I should never have come here. I am so sorry."

Zaaga placed a hand on hers and slowed her erratic attempts to stuff things into her bag. "You can go nowhere until the morning, so there is no point in doing that now," she said simply.

"May I borrow a horse?" Katy asked desperately. "I can't afford to pay for it, at least not now. Perhaps, if I explain it, the Jellicoes will still want me to take the position as their help. I can pay you back. I will pay you back."

"I know you will, but no payment is necessary. Our mounts are not our belongings. They choose to stay with us, and so any mount we lend to you will return to us if it wishes. If it does not, it will stay with you or go back to the wild herds. I will have Aandeg choose a suitable horse for you, and he will have it ready at first light. I can ride with you to Iron Creek if you would like company."

"Oh," Katy said, surprised by such an offer. The idea that a wild horse might choose to be with humans wasn't something she'd thought possible, and it hadn't even crossed her mind that the horses she'd seen the Ojibwe riding might be wild. They all seemed so well trained, so well bonded to their riders. "Thank you, I would be most grateful for a guide."

Neither Katy nor Garrett slept well. Katy tossed and turned on her bed, longing for the morning when she would be able to get away from this place, to finally start her new life whether Garrett wanted her or not. She wasn't sure if staying in Iron Creek was for the best, but at the moment it was all she had. She could not be fussy or let her pride get in the way of her taking a good position and giving herself and her child some hope for the future.

Garrett, however, had fetched his mount and ridden straight to his herd. He did not even wish to return to his cabin and longed for the solitude that being up the mountain with only his sheep could bring him. He woke Dylan, the lad he'd hired to watch them, and sent him home to his mother, then unpacked his bedroll and stared up, watching as clouds swept across the sky. Garrett tried to empty his mind of everything that had just happened.

No doubt, Mrs. White would probably return to Minneapolis, perhaps even to Chicago. She'd most likely send a letter to another unsuspecting fool and lie to him, too, until it was almost too late. A more foolish man might be taken in by the sweet face and the clear green eyes that could look you in the eye and not show a hint that they might not be telling the whole truth. The poor sucker would no doubt regret ever posting an advertisement in the papers, as he now did.

THE NEXT MORNING dawned with a light fog hanging over the encampment. Katy frowned as she stepped outside and pulled her shawl tighter around her body to keep out the damp air. There was no sign of Garrett or his horse, Janus, and she knew she had probably seen the last of him. He would not return, and he would not forgive her for her deception. And there would be no joining ceremony today. But she refused to be beaten by his reaction. The truth had been plain to see for weeks. That he had chosen to ignore it was hardly her fault. She owed him nothing.

Zaaga joined her in the doorway. "Are you ready to go?" she asked. Katy nodded. "It is but a short ride to Iron Creek. I shall introduce you to your new employers and then return to my house at Devil Track Lake itself."

Aandeg approached them, leading a gray mare with a sidesaddle on her back and a palomino mare with nothing more than a rope halter. Katy wondered absently if this was the horse that Mr. Harding had mentioned in his letters. It certainly looked different from the stocky animals that the Ojibwe rode. Zaaga mounted her horse with a grace Katy would be glad of, while Aandeg helped her up. "I shall arrange for your trunks to be brought to you later today," he said.

"Thank you for your kindness," Katy replied, feeling sad that she would be parting company with these people who had treated her as one of their own. Other than those few brief moments when she'd first opened her eyes from her fever, she had never felt an ounce of fear, only their love. They had made her feel welcome, and so much more. She truly felt like she belonged here, though she knew now that could never come to pass. They were Mr. Harding's family—not hers. She must now find her way without Zaaga's kindness and wise ways, and without Aandeg's patience and good advice.

Zaaga escorted her to the Jellicoes' elegant townhouse. It looked vast to Katy after so long living in a birch bark shelter. But Mr. Harding had been right to think that she and the young couple would mesh. From the first moment, the two women were fast friends, and Mr. Jellicoe was obviously besotted with his wife and determined to give her all the help and support she needed. Neither seemed to mind one bit that Katy was with child—in fact, it was quite the reverse.

"I shall build you your own home," Mr. Jellicoe told her over supper that evening. "A young mother needs to have space to raise her child the way she wishes. It won't take long. There's a lovely spot, beyond the copse of trees you see there." He pointed to a small woodland area just in sight of the house itself. "There's a lovely view of the mountain."

At the mention of the place Katy knew was Garrett's home, she felt a pang of regret, but she could not afford to refuse the Jellicoes' generosity because of a love affair that had barely had a chance to take flight. She thanked them profusely and made her way up to her room. Her trunk had been delivered by a couple of the young men of the tribe an hour before, so she began to sort through her things. She hung her clothes in the armoire and set her knick-knacks upon the mantel, including a daguerreotype of Jacob. He looked so handsome in the small portrait. She kissed it before placing it beside her bed. "I miss you," she told him. "I wish I could just talk with you one more time."

As she tucked the empty trunk away in the attic, Katy

suddenly remembered the letter she had written to her parents. She had not seen it anywhere as she'd unpacked, and so she hurried back to her room and rummaged in her handbag and the carpetbag that she'd brought with her that morning. There was no point. There was nothing in either. She must have dropped it somewhere. At least that took away the decision of whether to mail it or not. If it was lost it could do no harm.

# CHAPTER 15

*E*arly November 1878, Iron Creek, Minnesota

Garrett's days continued as they always had before Mrs. White had become a part of them. They were lonely and quiet. He tried to convince himself he did not mind, but he did. He missed the Ojibwe, and he missed Mrs. White and her sunny, kind smile. After their altercation, he'd never expected her to honor the position he'd arranged for her in Iron Creek, so when Dylan returned a few days later with tales of the new young lady in town, Garrett had been taken aback.

But then again, she was unlike anyone he had ever known before, so it was to be expected that she would not behave like any other woman. She had some gall—or was it courage? As he thought about it, he became more and more sure that it was the latter. Katy was not a mean-spirited person; she simply knew she had to do all she could to ensure her child was safe and that she could care for it when it came. Katy had a position here. It made sense for her to take it rather than try to start afresh somewhere else. Even so, he was surprised that Mrs. White would be so bold as to remain in Iron Creek after all that had happened.

But the thought that she might have done just that meant that he had never been gladder that he spent so little time in town. He had no desire to bump into her by accident, so he was grateful to have Dylan, who was more than happy to go and fetch the supplies Garrett needed or run the errands he should be undertaking himself. He called himself a coward often for not facing her, but it was too soon. And all too much for him to bear. His heart and his head were at war, and he didn't wish to risk doing anything he might regret before he was sure of what he truly wanted.

Almost a month passed before something happened that meant Garrett had to head into Iron Creek himself. He'd never much enjoyed visiting the town, but as he made his way down the mountain, he had never been so nervous. Garrett could not understand why; Mrs. White meant nothing to him. He'd spent weeks convincing himself of that, and he was sure that he meant it. She was just another deceitful woman, and he was better off without her.

As he rode along Main Street, he saw a heavily pregnant blonde woman walking up ahead of him, a basket filled with vegetables and bread from the new bakery slung over her arm. She paused outside the general store, peered into the window, then went inside. Garrett hadn't realized he'd been holding his breath until he took a deep, gasping one after she'd disappeared. Maybe he wasn't as in control of his feelings for Mrs. White as he'd thought. He urged Janus to a canter and made it past the store before she emerged.

Katy looked up and down the street before she crossed it. She noticed a familiar-looking horse heading into the blacksmith's yard, but thought little of it as she had come to know most people in town since her arrival. Someone going to the blacksmith's was hardly an unusual sight.

After stopping briefly to check on the boys in their wide perambulator on the porch of the small row of shops, she joined Mrs. Jellicoe, who was in the seamstress' tiny shop, fetching the twins' christening gowns. The bell above the door jangled noisily as Katy went inside. Mrs. Jellicoe turned and grinned at her, holding one of the lace-trimmed garments up in front of her. "Aren't they perfect?" she asked, beaming.

"They are," Katy agreed. She smiled at Jeanette Green, who looked pleased by the compliment. "The boys will look adorable in them. We can only hope they will act in accordance."

Mrs. Jellicoe laughed, a light tinkling sound like a peal of tiny bells. She was petite and pretty, with dark curls and rosy cheeks. Katy had liked her from the first, and the woman had not minded one bit that Katy had a babe on the way. In fact, she seemed delighted that her boys might have a new playmate. Mr. Jellicoe had been true to his word and arranged for the town carpenter to build a cottage for Katy on the grounds of their grand house. The construction was almost complete, and Mrs. Jellicoe and Katy were now busy sewing at all hours of the night and day to make it homely.

Jeanette packed the gowns in velvet and placed them into a box so that they would not crease as Katy and Mrs. Jellicoe took them home. Mrs. Jellicoe settled her monthly accounts and then they went outside, fetching the boys and wheeling them as gingerly as possible along the street so as not to wake them. But as they walked past the gates of Alec Jenks' yard, Katy realized why the horse and rider had been so very familiar. Garrett emerged onto the street. He glanced at Katy and flushed bright red. Katy felt her muscles tighten and her teeth clench as she watched him nervously.

Garrett couldn't stop staring at Katy. He truly hadn't allowed himself to believe that she would choose to stay. Of course, he had heard that she had, but hearing such things and believing them were two very different things. He had not wanted to check if the rumors were true. He had not dared to come to town to be certain.

But there could be no denying it now. And, as well as obviously being very settled with Mrs. Jellicoe, Katy was positively blooming, her belly now so swollen that nobody could deny it—not even a man who didn't wish to see it. She must be very close to her time. Garrett watched as she put a hand to the small of her back. It was obviously getting harder for her to bear the weight of the child that had created such distance between them.

Janus grew a little frisky, picking up on the tension in his rider's body, nickering and neighing as he began to pace and turn. Garrett tried to hold him still, crooning softly to the anxious horse. Mrs. Jellicoe looked on anxiously, and Garrett wondered if she was concerned for her boys with a nervous stallion around or if she was wondering how this most awkward of meetings might go. He looked at Katy and tipped his hat. "Good day to you, ladies," he said, then spurred Janus to a trot and moved away from them as fast as he could.

Katy's hopes that some kind of reconciliation might be possible between herself and Garrett were dashed to smithereens as he rode away from them at a gallop. She bit her lip and did all she could to hold back her tears. Katy had not expected seeing him again to hurt so terribly. Mrs. Jellicoe reached for her, with her blue eyes full of concern. "Mrs. White, are you quite well? You've gone so pale."

"I'm sorry," Katy said, shaking her head as if trying to rid her mind of the moment that had just passed. "I had not expected it to be so hard to see him again."

"He is a proud man. I know I have said this to you on so many occasions since you came to us, but he will come around. I am sure of it."

"And I wanted to believe you and I think I had convinced myself that I did—until just now," Katy admitted. "I truly thought that with time, he might forgive me for not having told him. But it seems he never will."

Mrs. Jellicoe gave her a sad smile, and the two women made their way back to the Jellicoes' comfortable home. They unpacked their purchases, Katy storing the ham and grain in the pantry while Mrs. Jellicoe carefully hung the boys' christening gowns. Katy couldn't get the brief and painful encounter from her mind. She could feel a knot of emotion growing in her chest, making it hard for her to breathe. She needed to get away. If things would always be so hard, she had perhaps made the wrong decision to stay in Iron Creek.

"Would you mind if I take a walk? I'll only be gone for an hour or so," Katy asked once she had arranged everything carefully in the pantry. "I need to clear my head."

"Of course, go. Take as long as you need. I shall put the boys down for their nap," Mrs. Jellicoe assured her. "We can finish your curtains tomorrow."

Katy kissed the kindly woman's cheek. She would always be grateful to Garrett for finding her a position with Mrs. Jellicoe. Not only had it given her somewhere to go, it had given her the support she so desperately needed in these last days of her pregnancy. They were similar in age, and both enjoyed music and books, as well as having the same concerns that all young mothers shared.

She left the house and went left along the street before turning off along a narrow, tree-lined path that led down toward the creek that gave the town its name. There was a quiet spot where a bend created a large pool that she often went to when she needed to think. It wasn't a sunny day, so there would be few others down at the water's edge. It would be the perfect place to make the decisions that she knew she needed to make so she was ready to act once her child was born.

As she emerged from the shade of the trees and walked along the banks of the creek, Katy felt the tension in her body begin to ease a little. This idyllic little spot was so peaceful and calm. She settled herself down on the bank and pulled her thick woolen coat around her body tightly. There had not yet been snow, but everyone said it would come soon. Katy could see her breath in the air. It was cold, bitingly so sometimes, stinging at her cheeks and ears, but she did not mind that. The baby kicked her behind the ribs, winding her a little. She gasped and took a few deep breaths to try to manage the pain.

"You are such a strong little soul, aren't you?" she said to her belly, stroking it affectionately. "Just like your papa." She laughed ruefully. "But that wins us no friends, little one. I had such hopes, but everything has gone so very wrong."

The sound of hoofbeats on the path behind her made Katy turn away from the creek to see who was approaching. She was surprised to see it was Garrett on his beautiful stallion. She stood up. He paused when he saw her, and she realized he was about to turn his mount's head to leave. "Wait," she said, her voice cracking with the sudden rush of emotion she felt. "We cannot go on this way."

He stared at her; no, *through* her. Katy shivered. His expression was so cold. "There is little to say, so why prolong this?" he said tightly.

"Little to say? How can you think that?" Katy protested. "We find ourselves in a small town and at odds. We need to resolve this for everyone else in town's sake, don't you think?"

"I rarely spend time in town. You know that. There is nothing between us that should concern anyone else."

Katy was speechless. Yet there was something in the fact that he was still there. He had not turned and left, and he did not believe what he was saying either, she was sure of it. "I am sorry I did not tell you of the child earlier." Katy started tentatively. "But you told me that you only wished to help me to find a new place to be, that you would be my friend. I know that things changed while we wrote to each other, and especially at the camp as we grew closer, but anyone with eyes could have seen that I was pregnant."

Garrett frowned. She was right. He had seen only what he wished, and he had thought on it so many times, knowing that his anger was misplaced, yet he could not let it go. He did not know why it hurt him so very much. "Mrs. White, you are right. I should have seen. I chose not to. But that does not change the fact that you omitted to tell me from the first," he said tightly. It was all he had to fall back upon, that original lack of honesty. He had been attracted to the simple truths she had laid out in that first letter and could not reconcile the fact she had mentioned everything else, but never that.

"Mr. Harding, much could have happened between that time and this," she said pointedly. "When I first wrote to you, I was not even certain that I was with child. I had my suspicions, but there were many other reasons why I might not have experienced my courses—lack of food, the grief of losing my husband, and fear for my own future. I told you of the troubles I lived through, and that I had to escape them. I explained that I might not make the best wife to any man, given I had only recently buried the man I loved so much that I left everything I had ever known behind to be with him."

Garrett knew that she was right, of course. And that just made him more stubborn. He did not enjoy being reminded that she had been honest with him when she'd said she was not writing to him because she longed for a husband but because she needed somewhere to run to. And indeed, he had offered her just that. He had told her that he would hold her to nothing, that he would be her friend. As such, there was no need for her to tell him anything further until she was happy to do so.

"You can believe this, or not," Katy continued, her eyes beseeching him. "But as we grew closer in our correspondence, I longed to tell you but did not know how to. It seemed too important to put in writing. I felt it important to say such a thing to your face and had every intention of doing so as soon as we met. But as you know, that did not go to plan either. I was so sick when we met that I could not tell you anything."

Katy's heart was heavy, but it lifted a little when Garrett dismounted. He hitched Janus to a nearby tree. The horse dipped his handsome head and began cropping the grass. Garrett took a few steps closer. Katy bit at her lip nervously. "You are right," he said softly. "You could not have told me anything when you arrived in Minnesota."

Katy shifted her weight onto her left foot. Standing was so hard now. The baby weighed heavy and low in her belly, preparing for its arrival in the world. But she could not bring herself to sit. She looked into Garrett's eyes. He looked so tortured. She had clearly hurt him very badly, and she could not possibly have known, but her actions must have reminded him of his lost wife and her infidelity. "I am sorry," she repeated. "I never meant to cause you any pain."

He shook his head. "It is not your fault," he admitted. "You could not have known about everything that had gone before as I did not tell you." He gave a wry smile. "I suppose I am as much to blame when I think about that. I should have told you more of my past, but I did not."

"Perhaps neither of us is to blame," Katy suggested tentatively. "After all, we were barely getting to know each other. Maybe we did everything too quickly, agreed to things before either of us was ready for them." She winced as the dull ache in her back spread through her pelvis in a wavelike motion.

Garrett did not miss the sign of obvious discomfort. "Are you alright?" he asked. "Is it the babe?"

"I think it is just an early warning. The midwife told me that you can get the signs early and that they pass."

"How long have the pains been happening?" Garrett asked, his face full of concern.

"Most of this morning," Katy said. "I'm sure they will pass. I need not worry until my waters break."

"Perhaps, but I think it might be wise for you to see the midwife—or maybe my mother—to be sure."

Katy laughed, amused by the typical male reaction to anything they did not understand. "I can assure you I am quite well."

"Even if that is true, perhaps we need to get you back to the Jellicoes," he said. "It is too cold for you to be standing around out here like this."

"I'm fine," she said, amused and touched by his obvious anxiety. "Women have been having babies for many years. There is nothing to be concerned about." His face clouded over, and Katy could have kicked herself. Of course, many things could go wrong, and he knew all too well that giving birth was one of the most dangerous things a woman could do.

"I am sorry. I didn't think," she said, reaching out a hand and placing it on his arm.

He took her hand in his and held it. His palms were so warm and hers were so cold. It sent shivers through her to be so close to him once more, but he assumed she was cold. He frowned. "It is time to get you inside. I will not take any further argument."

She let him help her up onto Janus' back, absurdly distracted by the way her body reacted to being pressed up against his tall, muscular body. When he stepped away, she felt colder than she had before. Her teeth began to chatter as he unhitched Janus and led Katy and his horse back to the Jellicoes' house in town. When he lifted her down, she lost the world around her once more, able only to focus on the scent of his skin and the feeling of his muscles against her hands and body.

He stepped away from her abruptly. Katy sighed and stepped up onto the porch. She turned back to him. "Can we start again? As friends?" she asked him.

He gave her a rather sweet, lop-sided smile. "I would like that," he said. "Perhaps I can bring the wagon down and take you to see my mother tomorrow? I know she would like to know how you are."

"And you would like to know that she thinks I am well," Katy said with a knowing smile.

Garrett chuckled, amused that she had seen behind his ruse. He would do well to remember that she was no fool. He bowed politely and made his goodbye, feeling lighter than he had in weeks. It felt so much better to have cleared the air between them. He would be glad to be her friend, though holding her so close had reminded him all too clearly that his body still had not forgotten its attraction to her. They had much to work through, and he surprised himself by praying that they would manage to do so.

# CHAPTER 16

id-December 1878, Devil Track Lake, Minnesota

It felt good to be at the Ojibwe winter camp once more. Though Zaaga had told her she would always be welcome there, Katy hadn't thought that the older woman had truly meant it. She had stayed away since she had parted with Zaaga. It had felt easier that way. But now she was able to spend time there again, back among her friends, Katy wished she had visited from the start.

Zaaga had seemed delighted to see her again when Garrett had brought her a couple of weeks previously. She had invited her back warmly, whenever Katy wished to visit with her. Katy wasn't foolish enough to think this was simply for the pleasure of her company. Zaaga was one of the very few people that Garrett trusted, and it seemed that he wished to be sure that Katy was well. She was sure that his agreeing to take

Katy for regular visits with the knowledgeable and skilled healer was to put his mind at ease, as much as it was for Katy and Zaaga's pleasure. The thought gave her considerable hope.

Katy learned much from Zaaga, from the best herbs to ease false contractions, to herbs that would help bring in her milk. She also taught Katy how to swaddle the babe to comfort it, and equally important, how to let the child be free to stretch and kick its legs so it would grow strong. She took some of her newfound skills back to Mrs. Jellicoe, who found the information and recipes the older Ojibwe woman sent unusual but very useful.

As her time grew nigh, Katy found it harder and harder to do much. She longed to sleep, though she struggled to get comfortable and had to rest more often during and between tasks to catch her breath. Mr. and Mrs. Jellicoe were happy for her to take as much time off as she needed, but Katy felt bad that she was not living up to her obligations and often tried to push herself too hard. So, her days at the camp became an oasis of peace and calm, where all Zaaga asked of her was that she help prepare or sort herbs around the fire in her small but comfortable home.

"How did you come to adopt Garrett?" Katy asked Zaaga one afternoon.

"Has he not told you?" the older woman asked with a fond smile.

"He has told me little about anything. He does not talk much about the things that matter to him," Katy said sadly. They might now be friends, but there was no sign that there might ever be anything more than that between them. He made polite small talk with her each time he came with the wagon to bring her to Devil Track Lake but never talked of anything important. Yet she knew that his concern for her was real. Otherwise, why would he want her to see his mother so often?

"He has always kept his thoughts close," Zaaga agreed. "I wonder if that was why Oma struggled to know how he truly felt about her. I wonder if things might have been very different had he spoken to her more."

"But she chose to be untrue," Katy asked.

"It is easy to see it that way." Zaaga paused as if trying to think about how to explain things to Katy. She pursed her lips and furrowed her brow for a moment. "To your people, marriage is a binding vow, especially for women."

"Yes, men's infidelity is often overlooked, even condoned, but a woman's could never be."

"Indeed," the older woman said as she swept the floor of the shelter. "Men in your world wish to know that a child is their own. Your rules of property and inheritance make such things important, I suppose."

Katy nodded. No man wanted to be betrayed, and no man wished to raise another man's child. "But Garrett was raised here, among the Ojibwe," she said. "Surely his beliefs should be those of the tribe?"

"And I think he thought they were. But he had spent time among his own kind, and learned their ways, by the time that Oma was carrying her child."

"But surely the Ojibwe frown on such things, too? If one is married to another, haven't you made a commitment to always choose them?"

"We do not always hold to a marriage being just one man and one woman," Zaaga admitted. She opened the door and swept the dirt she'd accumulated outside, letting in a gust of cold air. Katy shivered and pulled a nearby fur over her lap. Zaaga shut the door and smiled. "And it is important to know that divorce is easier here—and can be granted to both man and woman if they require it. I think we are aware that marriages arranged by one's family do not always work out as might be hoped. But Garrett and Oma made the choice themselves, which is not normally our way."

"They were a love match?" Katy asked, intrigued.

"Yes, they were inseparable from when they were very young. I doubt we could have convinced either of them to marry anyone else had we tried, and few would have wished to come between them if we had insisted upon a different match."

"That makes it even sadder, does it not?"

Zaaga sighed. "It does," she admitted. "Despite all my love, my boy had his own troubles. Oma's love could never have been resolved. Waabshkizi did not know where he belonged, and I think that took its toll on his relationship with Oma." She paused to make Katy a cup of raspberry leaf tea, then sat by the fire beside her. "He was always off somewhere alone. He would brood over the tiniest concerns, believing them to be because he was not one of us. Yet he was the only one who ever thought that way. I don't think anyone else ever saw him as anything other than my son."

"It must have been quite a burden to bear," Katy said, nodding her head as she tried to imagine a young white boy coming to terms with his new life in a strange place, among people who were not his family. "He was old enough to remember, was he not, that he was not born to you?"

"He was almost five, so yes, he was old enough to remember his first family and the life he'd had before he came to me. I always hoped my love for him would be enough. But it was not. He spent longer and longer away from the tribe and came back angrier and more unhappy each time. In the beginning, Oma went with him, but as time went on, she could not bear to see him drinking and gambling, living a life so far from the one he had here."

"I can understand that. It must have been hard for her to think that she was not enough. But why not divorce him before taking a lover?" Katy asked.

"I don't think she meant for that to happen," Zaaga said sadly. "I think she began to spend more time with Dibikad because he was Garrett's closest friend. I think by being with him, Oma felt that she was somehow with Garrett even when he was far away. I think it happened by accident. And I am sure Garrett felt the same way. He certainly never blamed Oma for anything. Dibikad could not forgive himself. He went to live with another tribe because he could not bring himself to stay here."

Everything Katy had learned about Garrett's past was so very sad. A child left orphaned so young, to be raised in a world completely different from anything he must have known beforehand. And then later, not only had he lost his wife and her child, he had lost his dearest friend, too. The matter of the child's parentage suddenly seemed to be the smallest aspect of this sad saga. She had the strong feeling that it was something that would have been forgotten and forgiven if only Oma had not passed away. She had left behind a gaping hole in the lives of two men who had loved her. The two could not even console each other in their grief, anger, and guilt.

"Zaaga…" Katy started, then stopped. She had wanted to ask if Garrett might ever forgive himself enough to love again, but it seemed such a trite question to ask after everything that had gone before.

"I don't know if he will ever forgive or forget," Zaaga said sadly, as if reading Katy's mind. "I don't know if he will ever stop punishing himself, but I do hope he will. When he first brought you to us, I hoped that he had finally managed to do so, but it seems that it only brought the worst memories back to him."

It wasn't the answer Katy had hoped for, but it was the one she had expected. She feared that there was no hope for them though she knew that, despite everything, she still cared for Garrett deeply. If he did not want her for his wife, there seemed to be little point staying in Iron Creek. She would be better off returning to Minneapolis, or possibly even Chicago, where there might be more chances of employment and perhaps the possibility that she might forget the troubled man that she had fallen in love with.

Garrett arrived late in the afternoon to take Katy back to town before it grew too dark. Zaaga convinced her son to stay for dinner with the tribe, as it could be some time before Katy would be able to visit again. Katy gave him a hopeful smile. She knew her time was drawing close. The strange pains she'd been having were growing stronger and happening more often. She felt ready and though she wished Zaaga would be able to be present at the birth, she knew it would be more likely to happen while she was in Iron Creek.

Garrett agreed, though he was concerned about driving the wagon in the darkness. "We must go as soon as we have eaten," he said sternly to Katy as if it was her that might delay them for some reason.

"Thank you," she said. "I may not be able to come again until after the little one makes an appearance, so I am glad to spend all the time here I can now."

"You have truly come to enjoy my mother's company," Garrett said, with a rare gentle smile. "I am glad of it."

"She is very wise and has taught me much," Katy admitted. "I would trust her with my life."

"I think there are many who feel that way," Garrett said proudly. "She is sought after for every birth, death, and moment of ill health in between by tribes all over the region."

As the evening went on, Garrett felt his nerves ease. It was clear that Katy was well-loved in the camp. She did her best to help, but watching her waddle to fetch things for his mother made Garrett laugh. Katy knew that she looked ridiculous and pulled faces at him as if to exaggerate it. She was a delight, and he regretted all that had gone wrong between them. He had been a fool to think that she would ever do what Oma had done. She might not have told him the truth straight away, but she had not kept it from him, and she had not cheated on him. The child was her husband's. There was no other man who might lay claim to it. But in all other ways, it would be the child of whoever was lucky enough to be Katy's husband in the future.

He tried to see the world as Katy might, and it made him even more impressed with her acceptance of a situation that few women would wish to experience, much less make themselves a real part of. He knew that his mother had taught her to cure leather and some herbal lore, and that Katy had been a keen student. She had made friends with many of the young women of the tribe, gravitating naturally to those who were pregnant like her or had young infants. She fitted in here, in a way he never really had. It made him wonder. Was that feeling he did not belong here, or anywhere, something he might change? If Katy could choose to be a part of all this as well as being a part of her own world, why could he not do the same? And if he could do that, would he perhaps find a way to feel that he deserved happiness with her?

# CHAPTER 17

id-December 1878, Iron Creek, Minnesota

The Jellicoes were preparing for Christmas with painstaking precision. They were determined that every part of their twins' first yuletide would be special. Katy and Mrs. Jellicoe had spent the first week of December searching the local woodlands for evergreens and winterberries, which they decorated the house with in a lavish display. As the day drew closer, Mr. Jellicoe prepared mulled wine and cider, slaughtered a turkey and plucked it ready for the big day, and spent many hours in the barn out the back, hammering and sawing at some mystery gift for the twins. Everyone in Iron Creek seemed excited for the upcoming celebrations, especially the Christmas Eve carol service to be held in the town's little church.

Katy struggled more and more as her time drew nearer, though she was sure the child was late in coming. Zaaga had reassured her that a baby will come in its own good time, and that if it wished to stay in its warm cocoon a little longer, it wasn't anything to be concerned about. But she wasn't the one with swollen ankles and almost constant back pain. Katy wished for it all to be over. As the days ticked by, she grew more and more afraid that something had happened to her little one, and when the child seemed to stop moving, she was distraught. To have come so far, to have endured so much—she could have borne none of it without the promise of Jacob's child.

Katy did not see Garrett again after her final visit to the Ojibwe. She was surprised at how much she missed him. He had become a quiet but reliable presence in her life, always happy to take her to see his mother and pick her up and see her home again safely. She had moved into the little cottage the Jellicoes had built for her some way from the main house, so she might have some privacy when she wasn't working.

Garrett sent her a rocking chair he had made, and it soon became her most treasured possession. But there had been no talk of anything more personal than how she fared. She knew no more of his heart now than she ever had, and she could not make any sense of him, though she longed to. Katy had not intended to fall in love with anyone; she had not believed it possible. She had loved Jacob so very much and had believed it would be impossible for anyone to replace him in her heart. Yet, though she knew she loved Garrett, she now knew that loving him did not mean that he had taken Jacob's place in her affections. She loved them both in different ways, because they were very different men.

When her real contractions began early one morning, just a week before Christmas, Katy barely noticed the difference from the false ones she'd been having for weeks. She did her chores in the morning and prepared lunch for the twins, then fed them and set them down for their naps as she moved to prepare a cold plate for her supper. Her employers had taken the gig to the market in Grand Marais the day before to buy some last-minute gifts and spend a little quiet time together. Mrs. Jellicoe had been concerned that Katy's time might come while they were gone, but Katy had assured them she would be perfectly fine, that they should go and enjoy themselves.

She sliced some bread and was about to butter it when she felt a warm fluid trickling down the inside of her thighs. Katy looked down to see her waters breaking all over the kitchen floor. Immediately, she was relieved that her pregnancy was finally over, though that soon passed when she realized there was nobody there to help her, and she did not know how quickly things might happen from this point onward.

She hurried outside to see if there was anyone she might call on, but the streets were empty. She didn't dare go far. There was nobody with the twins, and if they woke up and nobody was there, then they would fret. Virtually the entire town had gone to Grand Marais for the winter market and fair. Then she heard the familiar clang of a hammer on iron coming from the blacksmith's yard. She waddled over a little self-consciously. She didn't know Alec Jenks that well, but she knew he knew everyone, and Garrett had once told her he was a man who could be trusted if she ever needed help.

The burly smith took one look at her and immediately

quenched the iron bar he had been working on and set it down. "It's your time?" he asked as he approached and put a huge but comforting hand on her shoulder. She nodded. "Garrett asked me to keep an eye open," he explained. "The Jellicoes went to market?"

"Yes, they won't be back until tomorrow. And Amy Garside, too."

"The midwife? She's gone away when you're so close to your time?" Mr. Jenks said incredulously. "Well, we've prepared for this. I'm to take you to Devil Track Lake," he told her gently. "I've got a wagon ready, just in case. I'll send a lad to tell Garrett, and he'll meet us there, no doubt."

"But what about the twins?" Katy asked him anxiously. She couldn't leave them alone in the house. And they'd be waking soon.

"My mother will watch them," Mr. Jenks assured her. "Don't you worry. Everything's been thought of. We've all been ready for this for weeks."

Katy doubted they would make it to the Ojibwe camp before the child came, but it seemed that everything had been decided for her without her even knowing of it. It felt strangely good to have someone take charge, and, despite her vastly expanded girth, Alec Jenks lifted her into the back of the wagon as if she weighed nothing. It was filled with all the cushions Garrett had purchased to take her to the Ojibwe when she'd been sick. He drove quickly but carefully and got her to the camp sooner than she'd expected. Zaaga took immediate charge of her.

Before long, she was settled into Zaaga's longhouse, with

the older woman bathing her brow and softly counting the time between the now agonizing contractions, surrounded by members of Garrett's family. Katy recognized Diindiisi, Garrett's sister, and his cousins. Some of the older women of the tribe also filed in as Zaaga went about her checks to see how far along Katy was.

Despite or perhaps even because of the audience, Katy knew she was in good hands. She listened to the gentle chanting of the women as they sat around the shelter, swaying gently. It was soothing and helped her to calm her breathing. The pangs came with increasing intensity and with less time between them for her to catch her breath, so Katy barely heard the sound of rapid hoofbeats outside when Garrett arrived, but she was delighted to see him burst into Zaaga's home and refuse to leave it again. "This is woman's work," his mother reminded him.

"And she would normally have her mother, her sisters — family of some kind—with her. All she has is me, not that I am much," he argued. "I'll not leave her alone."

His mother caressed his cheek gently. "She's not alone; she's with family. Have you not noticed that I am here, your sister is here, all of your cousins and aunts are here?"

He looked around. Garrett had not noticed the many women there for Katy. He nodded respectfully to them all, and they smiled at him, but it was clear that they thought he should not be in the birthing chamber. He could feel it in them. But he was not Ojibwe. Neither was Katy. Their ways did not have to prevail if it wasn't what she wanted, though he'd not be permitted to be present in the white world, either. It was a domain just for women, one that few men wished to be a part of.

He moved to her side. "Do you want me to stay? I know it isn't proper, but if you want me to, I will," he said to her softly. She moaned as another contraction hit, then managed to smile.

"No, I am in good hands," she said, reaching up to cup his cheek, then biting her lip as another contraction came hard.

"I'm sorry," he whispered into her ear as he brushed a kiss on her sweat-slick cheek. "I have been a fool. I love you." She looked at him with wide eyes, obviously stunned by what he'd just said, but she said nothing in response.

"Out," Zaaga said firmly, ushering Garrett from the shelter. He looked back at Katy's pale face and prayed that she would survive. There was so much left unsaid between them, and he couldn't bear the thought that he might not be able to say it to her. Garrett had not been there when it had been Oma's time, and he would regret that until the day he died. He knew that things probably wouldn't have been different even if he had been there, but he couldn't help thinking that she might have gained strength from knowing he was nearby. It might be too late for him now, but at least he had made sure Katy knew she was loved.

Katy stared at the door of the shelter long after Garrett had left. She barely noticed the contractions as they came closer and closer together, and she did exactly as Zaaga told her without thinking. All her thoughts were on the man who had just left the room. He had said he was sorry. He had told her he loved her. And now her heart was singing, though her mind was not entirely sure whether she had perhaps dreamed it all.

But before long, she could think of nothing but her baby. She pushed when Zaaga told her to and tried to catch her breath between each push that hurt so much she feared she might rip in two before the child was delivered safely. So, when the sound of a baby's cry rent the air, Katy almost didn't believe it could be hers. When Diindiisi, Garrett's sister, handed her the tiny infant wrapped in a thick wolf pelt, Katy sobbed. The child was the very image of his father. "Oh my, he's perfect," she said, stroking the baby's tiny fingers and toes.

"Yes, he is," Zaaga agreed. "Congratulations, Katy."

The flap of the door opened, though Katy had seen no one leave to tell those waiting outside that the birth was done, and Aandeg entered. He smiled at Katy and her son. "May I?" he asked her, reaching for the child. She nodded and let him take her boy. The old man's wizened face beamed with happiness at the sight of him. "He is strong," he noted, taking in the lad's kicking legs and loud, hearty cry. "And he is determined, I think, like his mama."

"I hope so," Katy said with a laugh. She looked past Aandeg and saw that Garrett had come back inside, too. He looked as though he had lived every minute of the birth with her, and his handsome face was ravaged by fear. Garrett didn't take his eyes from hers. She nodded to him, and he smiled back at her before glancing at the child in his grandfather's arms. Aandeg was looking over every inch of the tiny infant as if searching for an answer he just couldn't find.

"When a child is born to the tribe, the elders give them their name. It is important to choose the right one," Garrett explained to Katy.

"Oh, but..." she broke off. Garrett wondered if she'd presumed that she would be able to name her own child, as was the custom for the white man.

"His Ojibwe name," Zaaga added to reassure her. "Like you, like Waabshkizi-Mnidoo, your little one will straddle both worlds, will he not?"

"I...I don't know," Katy said, looking at Garrett. "Will he?"

"I hope so," Garrett said softly. "But we have a lot to think about before we are sure."

"And I have a lot to think about before I give this one a name," Aandeg declared, handing the baby back to Katy. "I will consult with the other elders. We will have the naming ceremony a week from now. I will announce his name then."

Katy was a little deflated it would be a week before she would find out the name of her child, but she was touched that the tribe intended to treat them as their own. The women who had borne witness walked slowly out of the shelter behind Aandeg. Zaaga and Diindiisi, cleaned up, and then took the dirty water and cloths out of the shelter, leaving Katy, Garrett, and the baby alone.

Garrett grinned at her. "You can call him whatever you like in the meantime."

"Would it be too much for you to bear if I were to name him after his father?" she asked him tentatively. "He is so like Jacob."

Garrett nodded. "He was your husband and your son's father. I know I cannot compete with the ghost of a man you loved so dearly." He meant every word, but it was still hard for him to say it.

"Thank you," Katy said.

"But it only matters if you are prepared to forgive me," Garrett added, reaching out to caress the baby's plump cheek. "If not, then you need never see me again, so my opinion will mean nothing."

"I am happy to forgive you," Katy said. "I should have told you. I hope you can forgive me."

"You have nothing to be forgiven for. You did all you could to ensure this little one's future. Any mother would have done the same. I just…" he trailed off, not entirely sure how much he should say. She must be exhausted. There was time to talk about everything when she'd had some rest.

"Your mother told me more," Katy said, putting her hand over his and giving it a supportive squeeze. "I think I understand. It must have been hard growing up here, knowing you were different."

"And I was different among my own people, too. It wasn't until I saw you here that I realized my feelings were changeable. You were happy to be a part of the community here, to treat everyone as you wished to be treated, and to welcome everything new and unknown with excitement rather than fear. I hope I'll be able to do the same, though it may take me some time to learn."

christmas Eve 1878, Devil Track Lake, Minnesota

Young Jacob fretted a little as the wagon rocked and swayed as Garrett drove the three of them to Devil Track Lake. Katy wondered if Aandeg had even considered that the day he'd designated as Jacob's Ojibwe naming day was such an important day in the Christian calendar. He probably hadn't, and why should he? But it meant a lot to Katy that her son would receive an Ojibwe name on a day that had always been one of her favorite days of the year.

She remembered how Jacob's father had done all he could to make it special after they'd left Katy's parents behind in Richmond. She had always missed them so much more at Christmas than she did at any other time, and he had always tried so hard to make up for that. This new reason to celebrate would do a lot to help keep her mind from those she missed.

The wagon came to a halt just outside the Ojibwe winter encampment. Katy peered out of the tarpaulins to see what had stopped them. There were sometimes trees in the path, or if there had been heavy rains, Garrett might need to lead the horses around the flooded parts. But there was nothing there, and no sight of Garrett, either. Jacob whined, so Katy sat back down and soothed him by rocking him gently and crooning at him. He was soon sleeping once more. She laid him in the reed basket that Zaaga had made for him just as Garrett jumped up into the back of the wagon.

"What is it?" she asked him. He gave her an odd look, and he looked so serious that Katy started to feel a little concerned. "Garrett, tell me now, what has happened?"

"Nothing," he said nervously. "Nothing has happened. But I wanted to speak with you alone, and there is always someone nearby, whether we are in town or with my family. This seemed to be the only place I might be able to have enough peace to say what I must say to you."

Katy waited patiently. Suddenly, Garrett didn't know how to say what he'd been practicing for days. He ummed and ahhed until she gave him a hard stare. "Garrett, whatever it is, can it really be so bad?" she asked.

"I do hope it isn't bad at all," he said, grinning nervously. "I know I have been a fool. I let my past come between us when I should have learned to live with it all long ago. I left you alone when you needed someone the most. I am just lucky that you are sweet and kind enough that you have found it in your heart to forgive me for that."

"Garrett, you have been by my side through everything,"

Katy said. "You even arranged for the townsfolk to get me to your mother should my time come when there was nobody there for me. I know you also asked Mr. Barclay and even Mr. Wilson as well as Mr. Jenks to have transport prepared at all times."

"Ah, you know about that," he said with a little chuckle. "I feared that perhaps I might have taken things a little too far."

"I will be forever grateful, because it meant that I was safely brought to bed with Jacob Junior. And it showed how much you were thinking of me, and the babe's safety. You know from painful experience how dangerous it can be."

Garrett flushed. She was being too generous, and he was losing track of what he had meant to say again. He took a deep breath. "Mrs. White, Katy, what I wanted to say—and I will understand if you say no given the way I have treated you—is, well, will you marry me?"

Katy stared at him. Garrett waited patiently. He could not read her face; there was no inkling as to how she had taken his question. He tapped his fingers on his thighs nervously, waiting for her to respond. She pursed her lips, looked down at baby Jacob, then back at him. "I think that would be lovely," she said, a cheeky smile escaping.

Garrett grinned. "You mean it?" he asked anxiously. "You truly can forgive me for being so stupid as to let you go before? I promise you I won't this time. In fact, I was rather hoping that we might make tonight a dual celebration—if I am not rushing you. Aandeg can join us, as well as complete Jacob's naming."

Katy laughed at his eagerness. "I think that would be perfect."

"Oh, Katy." He sighed happily.

"Dearest Garrett, I am so glad," she said. She leaned forward and pressed a chaste kiss to his lips. "Are you sure you will be happy to be a father to Jacob? You really want that?"

"Oh, I do, Katy," he said, pulling her close and claiming her lips for his own. "I truly do."

They laughed. Garrett reached into his pocket and pulled out a thin gold chain with a tiny crucifix upon it. "This was my mother's," he explained. "The one who birthed me. Zaaga took it from the wagon where she found me, along with the watch I always wear." He pulled out the silver watch and showed it to her. "I want you to have it as a symbol of my commitment to you."

Katy and looked it over. The necklace was simple and pretty, and it obviously meant a great deal to him. She was touched that he wanted her to have it. "Thank you," she said softly. "I shall treasure it."

Garrett glanced at the time on his pocket watch before popping it back into the pocket in his vest. "We will be late if we remain any longer," he said. "But you have made me the happiest man in Minnesota, Katy White, and one day I shall give this watch to our son. A gift from the grandfather he did not get to know." His words brought a tear to Katy's eyes, and she reached over and pressed a kiss on Garrett's cheek in gratitude for his acceptance of her son as his own.

Katy couldn't wipe the smile from her face as they

completed the last part of their journey, and she was still grinning when they arrived at Zaaga's longhouse. Garrett's mother welcomed them inside and cooed over baby Jacob's progress. She looked at them both closely. "Something has happened," she said. "Are you going to tell me, or do I have to guess?"

"I asked Katy to marry me again," Garrett said happily.

"And I said yes again," Katy added.

Zaaga stared at them both for a while, making Katy and Garrett feel uncomfortable. She looked so closely at them that it felt as if she was looking through their very thoughts. "Yes, you're both ready this time," she said at last, then embraced them both. "I am happy for you, my boy," she said to Garrett, kissing his handsome face. She turned to Katy. "And I am beyond glad you will be my daughter and that this fine young man will be my grandson." She took Jacob from Katy and covered his little face with kisses.

They made their way outside and ambled to the ceremonial ground. Zaaga's neighbors joined them as they walked. The rest of the tribe was waiting for them, standing around in a broad circle. Aandeg and the other elders were standing in the center. Above their heads, the northern lights flickered in glorious green, gold, blue, and all the colors of the rainbow. Aandeg called on the tribe to quiet down, then stepped forward and took Jacob from Zaaga, nodding to Katy and Garrett as he did so, and raised the boy up to the sky. "Tonight, we come together to welcome the newest member of the Ojibwe," he said, turning around so everyone present could see the baby clearly. "Until this very evening, his name escaped us.

But nature always tells us the way if we only open our eyes and our ears to see and hear her intent."

He lowered Jacob and held him against his chest. "In the name of his father and mother's people, he is Jacob. But to us, he will now be known as Waussi-Noodae." Everyone murmured their appreciation for the chosen name. Katy turned to Garrett, her eyes questioning.

"It means northern lights," he said with a soft smile. "He is named for the phenomenon that has welcomed him to this world."

"That's lovely," Katy said as Aandeg handed Jacob back to her. She kissed her son's soft forehead. "Waussi-Noodae," she whispered to him. "Welcome, my darling boy, to this world of wonders."

Aandeg shook Garrett's hand, then embraced him tightly. "You came to us a pale little thing, abandoned by those who had brought you into this world as they made their way to the spirit world. Your mother did all she could to send them safely on their way, and for so long, we feared you might join them. You were like a ghost for so long."

"And that is why you chose my name?"

"That is why I chose your name. But we may need to choose you a new one as you are no longer the wraith you once were. You have come home, my boy. You seem to have found yourself at last."

"I do believe that may be true," Garrett said with a wry smile. "But I'll not be parting with my name. Mother said that it came to you as soon as you saw me. That you never had any doubts. I should have always trusted you were right."

Aandeg smiled and embraced his grandson, obviously touched by his words. Then he drew back once more and looked at Katy. "But your wife-to-be needs to be welcomed into the Ojibwe, too, and receive her name." He encouraged Katy to hand Jacob to Garrett, took her by the hand, and led her into the circle. He led her past each member of the elder council, then turned back to the tribe. "You all know Katy White. She is one of the Ojibwe now. And so, we also welcome Minwaadizi to our number, the mother of Waussi-Noodae and the soon-to-be wife of Waabshkizi-Mnidoo."

Garrett stepped forward with Jacob cradled in one arm. He took Katy's hand and let his grandfather bind their hands together with a cloth made by Zaaga. In Ojibwe, he stated something that made the gathered crowd sigh contentedly. "Katy White, Minwaadizi, the kind one, I promise to love you for the rest of my days. I vow to care for you whether times are good or bad. We may straddle two worlds, but I now know that we are all one. I love you and choose you to be my wife."

Katy was touched by his words. "Make your vow to Waab-shkizi," Aandeg said softly.

"But I don't speak Ojibwe," Katy said, feeling suddenly nervous and a little foolish.

"You don't need to," Garrett said. "Everyone here speaks English."

"Then, I take you, Garrett Harding, to be my husband. I promise to love you, whether things are easy or hard. I vow to care for you whatever comes our way. I look forward to all the new discoveries we will make together. I love and choose you to be my husband."

Aandeg chanted for a few moments, occasionally touching their foreheads, then bound the cloth tighter around their hands. "In the eyes of the tribe, our ancestors, and all the spirits, under the lights special to our people, I bind you," he said with a smile at them both. "Be happy, and live in love and joy."

# EPILOGUE

 id-April 1879, Iron Creek, Minnesota
The spring blossoms were a beautiful sight. Katy sighed contentedly as she approached the creek and began to cut those she liked the best from the trees. She sang softly to herself. Katy was happier than she had been in a very long time. Mrs. Jellicoe had insisted that she and Garrett wait to be wed until he could build her a house at least as nice as the one Katy would be leaving to marry him. Katy had been reluctant. In her mind, she was already married to her handsome Ojibwe husband. But she had dreamed of a real wedding since she was a girl and she had not had one when she had married Jacob, so she had reluctantly accepted the order.

She bent over the perambulator and tickled her son under the chin. Jacob Junior was thriving, and he had bonded so well with his father that Katy doubted anyone would ever know that Garrett wasn't the child's birth father. He took the baby to see his Ojibwe family often, much to Zaaga and Aandeg's delight. Katy usually went with them, but from time to time, she enjoyed the few hours of peace and quiet that the two men in her life being gone offered her.

"After tomorrow, we will move to the house on the mountain," Katy said to her son. "You'll love living there with Daddy's sheep and Janus. The air is so fresh there, you can see for miles around, and we will be closer to the Ojibwe who love you so much." Jacob gurgled happily and reached for his toes, grabbing them with his surprisingly strong little fists. "I know. Why wouldn't they? You are very lovable." Katy grinned as she placed the blooms she had chosen on top of his blanket.

She turned the carriage around and pushed her son back toward Iron Creek. Main Street was as busy as always, and the stagecoach had just pulled in, so everyone was clamoring to see if there was a parcel or a letter on board for them. But Katy walked on serenely—at least she did until she saw an elderly couple descend from the carriage. Their hair was grayed, but she would have known them both anywhere. Her parents!

Unsure whether to hide or to rush forward to greet them, Katy wondered why they were there at all. How could they possibly know where she was? Had someone written to them? Perhaps Garrett had. He knew how much she missed them, but she doubted that he would do such a thing. He knew all too well that people had to come to their senses alone, as he had. Taking a deep breath and steeling her spine, Katy marched forwards, keeping the perambulator directly in front of her.

"Mam, Pa," she said as firmly as she could muster when she drew close.

"Katy," Mam said, her voice a mere whisper, her eyes filling with tears. "Oh, my little girl. You are so grown up."

Pa looked off to the side as if he couldn't bear to look Katy in the eye. "Pa?" she asked. "Aren't you at least going to look at me?" He turned, and Katy could see his Adam's apple bobbing frantically as he tried to hold back a surge of emotion. His eyes were filmed with tears, but he seemed determined not to let a bunch of strangers see him weep in public. "I think we should go somewhere and talk," Katy said, indicating that they should follow her.

She took them along the street to the Jellicoes' house. Mr. Jellicoe was at work and Mrs. Jellicoe had taken the twins to visit with her mother, so Katy knew the house was empty—at least for now. She showed them into the parlor, then went to the kitchen to fetch some tea. Her hands shook as she poured the water from the kettle into the pot, and she almost dropped the cups and saucers as she placed them on the tray. She could barely remember the last time she had felt so nervous.

She returned to the parlor to find her father anxiously pacing and her mother sitting by the fireplace, wringing her hands and looking as afraid as Katy felt. Katy set down the tray and poured each of them a cup of tea, adding milk and sugar. Her mother put hers down straight away. Pa took a sip, then another, before he did the same. Katy didn't even pick hers up.

"Why are you here?" she blurted, unable to take the tension any longer.

Mam pulled out a worn letter from her handbag. Katy's mouth fell open. It was the letter she had written in the back of the wagon. The one where she had spilled every feeling, every thought, every accusation, and every hard word she'd ever wanted to say to her parents for abandoning her. How on earth had they received it?

"This was not an easy read," Mam said, her Irish lilt more pronounced than usual due to the emotion in her voice.

"It was never meant to be sent," Katy said, hanging her head, mortified that they knew everything. "I thought it was lost. I wrote it simply to sort through everything in my head. It wasn't really for you."

"Well, that is by the by," Pa said. "We know it all now. Who sent it and whether you meant us to read it doesn't matter. We have read it. And you are right."

Katy's head jerked up. He'd never told her she was right in her life. He never apologized to anyone, never admitted he might be in the wrong. And here he was, after all these years, and he had said she was right. "I am?"

"You are," Mam said sadly. "I cannot tell you how many times we have regretted not supporting you all those years ago. We should have been there to see you wed. We should have been there to help you when Jacob was unwell. We should never have pushed you away."

Katy was stunned. She had dreamed of this moment from the day she'd left home all those years ago. All she'd ever wanted was her parents' blessing for the choices she had made —knowing all the dangers, but knowing she had to take those risks anyway.

"Jacob was the man you said he was," Pa said, and it was said generously. "I was wrong. I thought he'd abandon you as soon as things got tough. But he didn't. He worked hard. He supported you as he should have. And he loved you, didn't he?"

"Oh, Pa, he did," Katy said with a sigh. "He was a fine husband, and I am sure he would have been the most wonderful father had he lived to meet his son."

A cry from Jacob announced he had woken from his nap. Katy moved to where she had left the perambulator when they'd come in. She lifted him up out of his blankets and carried him toward her mother. "Mam, meet Jacob Junior," she said proudly.

Her mother reached out her arms and took the infant and cradled him, tears pouring down her cheeks as she covered his little face with kisses. "And aren't you a bonny lad?" she crooned.

Pa leaned over and caressed his soft head. "He is a fine young man," he said proudly. He turned back to Katy. "I am so sorry, lass. I…" he tailed off, unable to finish his thought as a wave of emotion overtook him and the tears he'd been holding back fell. Katy stepped forward and wrapped her arms around him. He hugged her back, and Katy felt whole again.

When the Jellicoes returned, they were more than happy for Katy's parents to stay as long as they wished, even offering them permanent use of the cottage they'd built for Katy if they wished to stay in town. With Mam and Pa settled in and Jacob in bed, Katy wandered out into the gardens and looked up at the full moon. She wondered if Garrett, at the new house, was looking up at it, too. He would hardly believe all that had happened when she told him.

THE FOLLOWING MORNING, the day of the wedding, dawned with rain pounding on the roof of the newly finished cabin Garrett had built. This new home had three bedrooms, a fine parlor, a vast kitchen, and a comfortable living room, with an outhouse within easy reach of the wraparound porch. He could hardly wait to bring his new wife and son home to it. Though Katy knew he'd been working all hours to ensure it was ready, she had not been permitted to visit.

He pumped water from the well and had a thorough wash before putting on his best suit and saddling up Janus. Garrett was about to head into Iron Creek when the sound of hoof-beats alerted him to the arrival of his family. Zaaga and Aandeg led almost the entire tribe of the Ojibwe toward him. He had never felt so much a part of them, and he was proud to have them all with him today. But one figure, on a black stallion that Janus recognized as easily as Garrett did, hung back. Janus strained to join his old friend, and Garrett let him guide him toward Dibikad.

"I heard you were getting married again," Dibikad said awkwardly.

"I am," Garrett said a little shyly. He had often wondered what he would say to his old friend if they were ever to meet again. He'd rehearsed all manner of speeches. Some gentle and forgiving, others harsh and brutal. Now he was just so happy to see his friend, he only wanted to embrace him and forgive him.

"I am sorry," Dibikad said sadly. "I have no defense and do not deserve your forgiveness, but I wanted to come today, to know that you had found happiness despite everything."

"I have," Garrett said. "And she has helped me to learn from my past. There is nothing to forgive my friend, my brother. I am glad you are here. Will you stand with me today? The white men always choose someone to be by their side. Will you be my best man?"

Dibikad looked relieved, then grinned. "I'd be honored," he said. "But please tell me I don't have to wear a suit like that." He took the lapel of Garrett's suit between his fingers and shuddered at the feel of the scratchy woolen fabric.

"Can you at least wear a clean pair of pants and a shirt?" Garrett joked.

"I can manage that," Dibikad said, and the two men laughed and embraced each other as if nothing had ever passed between them.

Escorted by his oldest friend and his family, Garrett made his way into Iron Creek once they'd located some clothes suitable for Dibikad to wear. All the townsfolk had come out to welcome them, and they lined the streets clapping and cheering Garrett as he approached the church. Garrett had been on the verge of tears ever since the Ojibwe had arrived at the cabin, but he struggled to hold the tears inside with this overt display of friendship. He shook hands and greeted everyone warmly.

The combined crowd of townsfolk and the tribe escorted

him into the church where he took his place at the altar, Dibikad at his side. The Jellicoes arrived last. An elderly lady was with them, carrying baby Jacob. She had graying hair, but her features were unmistakable. She was so like Katy that she could only be her mother, but how had that happened? He'd only seen Katy a few days ago, and she'd made no mention of her family coming—or that she was even in touch with them.

His questions would have to wait. His bride had appeared at the end of the aisle, clad in a green gown to match her eyes, on the arm of a proud-looking Irishman. She beamed when she saw Garrett, and he could not take his eyes off her as she made her way toward him. He barely heard a word of the ceremony as the minister spoke the words over their heads, but when they turned to each other to make their vows, he repeated them with a clear voice, hoping that Katy would know just how much he meant every word. She spoke her vows with just as much fervor, and in no time at all, they were well and truly man and wife.

They made their way outside, where Garrett kissed Katy soundly. "Thank you for changing my life," he said.

"Thank you for giving me a new life," she said, smiling up at him.

"Why didn't you tell me your parents were coming?" he asked.

"I didn't know. They arrived yesterday, out of the blue," Katy said happily. "It was the very best surprise. I can only assume that it was not you that sent them my letter if you did not know that they might be coming?"

Zaaga, standing nearby, blushed. "It was me," she admitted. "I found it after you'd left for Iron Creek, and I didn't mean to, but I read it. When I saw how much pain losing them had caused you, I knew, as a mother, that they would want to know—that they would want to put everything right if they could. Forgive me if I did the wrong thing, but I sent them the letter."

Katy flung her arms around the older woman. "I cannot thank you enough," she said.

"And neither can we," Katy's pa said, grinning. "You were right. We needed to know the pain we had caused. We believed that we were doing the right thing, but it cost us our daughter. Never again."

Katy hugged him as Garrett took Jacob from her mother, then she hugged her before she turned to Dibikad. "I have not met you but given how many people from the past this wedding seems to have attracted, I can only assume that you are Dibikad. I cannot tell you how happy I am to meet you and to know that all has been forgiven." He blushed as she embraced him but hugged her back gladly.

"Please don't try to steal this wife," Garrett said, his face impassive.

Dibikad blanched, then, seeing Garrett's laughing eyes, laughed with his old friend. "I don't think my own wife would be too happy with me if I did," he said. "Will you come and meet her soon? She is with child and travel is too much for her now."

Garrett and Katy looked at each other and smiled, thinking of all she'd gone through during her pregnancy with Jacob.

But it had been worth it, and she would do it all again in a heartbeat. "We would love to," she said.

The crowd of family and friends escorted the couple up the mountain to their new home. Katy gasped when she saw how lovely it was. She and Garrett waved everyone off, and finally, the three of them were alone on the porch.

"I love you, Mrs. Harding," Garrett said, taking her in his arms and kissing her passionately.

"I love you, Mr. Harding," she replied.

"And I am honored to be your father, little one," Garrett said to Jacob, kissing the top of the baby's downy head. "You came as quite a surprise, as did your mother and her tenacity, but I don't wish to be without either one of you now. You helped me to find my way home, and it turns out, it was never a place. Home is the people who I love and who love me. I will always be grateful to you for bringing me home."

The End

## OTHER SERIES BY KARLA

Sun River Brides

Ruby Springs Brides

Silver River Brides

Eagle Creek Brides

Iron Creek Brides

# CONNECT WITH KARLA GRACEY

Visit my website at www.karlagracey.com to sign up to my newsletter and get free books and be notified as to when my new releases are available.